Love You Tomorrow

KATELYN SIMEONE

LOVE YOU TOMORROW

And now you are
And I am
And we're a mystery
Which will never happen again.
—E. E. CUMMINGS

CONTENTS

———

CHAPTER ONE

Awake

AND SUDDENLY, I opened my eyes. I couldn't make out much about my surroundings. I could see a window out of the corner of my eye, about a foot away from my bed. The window was made of safety glass that had a thin metal wire running crisscross throughout. Beside the window was a wooden door with a metal handle that led out into a hallway. My hearing was quite muffled but I noticed the faint beeping of what sounded like a heart monitor. I turned my head slightly to the right and could see a shadowy figure of a man standing on the other side of the window. I heard a muffled version of his voice. He was clearly frantic as he ran from the window but his exact words were unclear to me. I felt a heavy pain in my chest and realized there was some sort of tube in my throat and mouth. I couldn't make much of the world around me, so I just closed my eyes and went back to sleep.

I woke up again with five people surrounding my bed. All of them were dressed in blue scrubs, and I could not make out any of their faces. One of them raised their hand and signaled for everyone to back away from me. They all slowly backed up while the room began spinning. The muffled beeping of the machines next to me made me somewhat nauseous and I couldn't move a single muscle no matter how hard I tried. I closed my eyes as the feeling of nausea overtook me again and my hearing cut out. I felt my heart thumping hard in my chest and when I opened my eyes, all five people were back at my bedside. They were all moving frantically but the room was spinning once again, so I shut my eyes and went back to sleep...

———————

I OPENED MY eyes once more, rested my hand on my forehead, rubbed my eyes and opened them again. The dim light was quite refreshing; my eyes were watering from...whatever was going on before. I took my hands away from my eyes and let them flop to my sides. Now that I could see and think at the same time, I realized I must be in a hospital.

I looked to my right and saw the window again. The blinds were mostly closed, with little rows of light beaming through. The hallway on the other side of the window was quite bright, but quiet. Next to my bed was a small tray table. The ceiling above me was the typical white hospital ceiling with little black holes pierced throughout the tiles. I always thought hospital rooms were so ugly because of how much white there is, but I didn't mind what I'd seen of this one so far because I could make out a smiley face in the little holes in the ceiling tiles. I like finding smiley faces because sometimes they are the only form of acceptance I receive. It makes me feel as if the universe is happy I'm here.

Four long lights hung from the ceiling, all off. I followed the second hanging light down to the wall opposite me. There hung a whiteboard with all of my information on it. The board was quite colorful. The top of the board read "My Care Board" with the date, Friday, December 15 (...wait, is that right?). The hospital phone number was displayed in black marker: (631) 477-1000. Below that, it read "My Name Is: Adelynn Grace Davis, My Room Number Is: 829." Below that three names were listed: "My Nurse Is: Crystal, My Nurse Assistant Is: Marissa, My Physician Is: Dr. Burke."

Below the names of my doctors was all of my dietary information, along with the letters K.E. I instantly got queasy—that meant whatever happened to land me in this place was bad enough for me to need a feeding tube. I remember learning about the different types of diets in my biology class. When I learned about feeding tubes I never paid too much attention because I knew I was way too cautious to ever get myself into a situation where I needed one. What got me into this position is still unclear. I began thinking about hospitals and how uncomfortable they make me. I have always been extra cautious in sports growing up because I hated having to visit hospitals and the one way to avoid going to one is by simply not getting hurt.

I focused back on the board and noticed the next few columns were small and had limited but important information. The words "high fall risk" were circled in bright red marker and the words "low mobility" were written next to that. The board noted in the next column that my plan for the day was to get better and that my parent's discharge was pending—whatever that meant. Above the board was a massive TV that was turned off. At least I can watch my favorite shows while I am here.

I was looking at the foot of my bed when I noticed a man sitting there—my dad. He was on his phone, as usual. He didn't even realize that I was awake. I didn't pay too much attention because this was very typical of him. The big New York businessman was there to support his daughter when she was hurt—in reality, he was working the whole time he was in the hospital room and didn't even care to glance over every few minutes to see if she was even still breathing. Over his shoulder I noticed the color of the wall. The hospital room was a very pale yellow. I caught sight of the little hills my feet made in the blanket out of the corner of my eye and wiggled my toes. I had little feeling in my body but I could wiggle my toes and my fingers.

To my right was a massive window to the outside world. I looked out and saw the skyline of New York City. I've always disliked living on Long Island, even though I grew up there, but the one thing I love is the city. I love how anonymous the city makes me feel. When I go there I feel like no one cares and I like that feeling. I stared at the skyline for what felt like forever, but it was very comforting. In fact, I wouldn't have minded staying in that hospital room forever if it meant I got to see that view of the city every night.

I began thinking about how badly I wanted to walk the streets of New York again. Reminiscing on the time that I went to the city with my mom when I was younger. We went ice skating at the Rocke-feller Center ice rink on Christmas Eve. I was six at the time and didn't know it yet, but we were in the city that night because she and my father were having marital problems. We stayed in a hotel from the week of Christmas up until New Year's, when my mom and I watched the ball drop right from our hotel window. My favorite trait about my mom is how she can make the best out of any situation. I've noticed I inherited that trait from her, especially recently. I mean here I am sitting in a hospital bed with my father not even caring that I'm awake, but I am lying here looking at the skyline.

Suddenly my thoughts were interrupted by the opening of the door and a woman's voice. I turned my head and saw a woman that looked to be no more than twenty-five. She had short blonde hair, a light complexion, dark eyes, and a soft smile. She was wearing a pair of blue scrubs with her name emblazoned on the pocket of the shirt. Her name is Marissa; the board above my father's head indicated that she was my nurse's assistant.

"Well look, someone is finally awake." She walked towards my left and continued, "Hi Adelynn, my name is Marissa and I am your nurse's assistant. Every night that you are here I will be here and I'll also stop by during the day if Crystal needs help."

"It's nice to meet you, Marissa," I said, with a slightly shaky voice.

"Don't worry, I won't make you talk long; I don't want to exhaust your vocal cords. I just wanted to introduce myself and let you know what was going on. You were brought in last week from a car accident that occurred late on Friday night. You didn't have too much physical damage, but you did have some trauma to your head. You fell into a coma; we had to give you a feeding tube to make sure that you got the proper nutrients because we didn't know how long you would be under. We're probably gonna have to keep you here for a few days and run some tests to monitor your brain activity and make sure you're healed enough to go home. We're also going to give you a therapist that you will meet with periodically at the request of your father just to make sure that no new mental health concerns have arisen due to the physical trauma your brain suffered. You've got this red button at your bedside that will alert me or Crystal when you press it. If you need anything feel free to alert us and we will come check on you. I'm gonna begin checking your heart rate and just do some other standard checks while I am here. Do you have any questions for me?"

I shook my head.

"Great! I'll begin those checks now," Marissa said as she turned towards the machine next to my bed and clicked a button.

My father had looked up when Marissa walked into the room and acknowledged her presence. He was only partially listening to what she was saying, which isn't uncommon for him. As soon as she was done speaking with me, he was back to being completely absorbed in his phone.

Marissa grabbed the clipboard at the end of my bed and walked back over to the machine. She began writing on it and I began thinking about what she said. A car accident? I don't remember getting into a car accident; actually the last thing I remember is going to bed last Thursday night. I didn't quite know how to feel or react. Was I alone in the car? Why is my father not more concerned? Where's my sister? My mom? Either of my stepparents? I mean, I know my family isn't very tight-knit but they can't even come to visit me in the hospital? My father quickly stood up, interrupting my thoughts.

"Mariah, is it?" he asked as he looked up at her.

"It's Marissa," she responded as she turned around.

"Are you gonna be here for a while, I have to head out," he stated.

"Yes. If I am not here for Adelynn, Crystal will be."

"Great," my father said as he turned towards me. "I have to run some errands for work Adelynn. Elizabeth will be here in the morning to check on you."

I nodded as he waved at me and walked out the door. Not even a kiss on the forehead or an "I love you." I guess nothing has changed.

"Who is Elizabeth?" Marissa asked while clicking buttons on the machine.

"She's my stepmom," I answered.

Marissa was hooking the blood pressure monitor up to me so she just nodded at first. She responded a few seconds later with, "Oh that's nice! Do you like your stepmom?" I answered with a nod that Marissa saw out of the corner of her eye; she acknowledged it with a soft smile.

The truth was I was lying. It's not that I don't like Elizabeth; I just don't necessarily enjoy her company. It's clear the only reason she is with my father is for his money. She and I don't have any problems with each other, we just aren't close. She began dating my father about six years ago. Within two months she had moved into our house and she was already planning their wedding. Seriously, Elizabeth had their entire wedding planned out before my father even proposed to her. My father didn't even ask me or my sisters if we were okay with her moving in, or with him replacing Mom so quickly when he *did* propose.

They got married the following summer, and the ceremony was beautiful, but I wasn't part of it in any way whatsoever. Neither were my sisters. My eldest sister, Harper, didn't seem to mind because she had her newborn son, Westin, to take care of. My sister Victoria and I however, were just sitting there watching this new woman take our mom's place in our father's life. I'm in one wedding photo, and that's the group photo that we took at the end of the reception. On the bright side, my father was not paying any attention to Victoria and I, and we were able to sneak a few drinks from the bar. They helped relieve the uncomfortable vibe I'd been getting the entire day.

After my father's wedding, he and Elizabeth went on a three-week trip to Europe, leaving us at our mother's house because Victoria and I were only in our early teens and not nearly old enough to be home alone for three weeks straight. During their honeymoon, my father never called either Victoria or me, not even once. I guess he was too busy with Elizabeth, but I don't believe that to be true. He was probably working on his honeymoon and forgot that Victoria and I even existed because we weren't physically in front of him at that exact moment.

My mom, of course, was not too thrilled by my father moving on so quickly, but didn't seem to care too much. She hid her feelings about my father until last year; then she began telling me how she *really* felt about him. My mother hates my father so much that she will no longer let us go by his last name, Davis, when we are in Michigan. Mom has since remarried to a man that I actually really like. His name is David and he makes her genuinely happy. The first time I met him, he took Victoria and I bowling. I won and he bought me ice cream as a reward. To the eighteen-year-old me I am today that's no big deal, but to the eleven-year-old me, that was like my whole world. They got married two years ago and had a very small, casual wedding and they had both Victoria and I as the ring bearers. We were in every single photo taken at the wedding and I genuinely had a fun time. David's last name is Carter, so we go by Carter when we are there.

My parents' divorce wasn't messy; it was simply just uncomfortable I guess you could say? My father was (and still is) a workaholic. My mother is a teacher, so her schedule matched up with ours quite well, but my father was just always working. That Christmas we spent ice skating at Rockefeller Center, my mom got upset with him a few days before because he picked up shifts on Christmas Eve and Christmas itself. My mom got mad and left with me and Victoria, dropping Victoria off with Harper and taking me to the city. Within about half a year, the divorce was finalized. My mother was living in the house next to Harper. She had joint custody, but our father was the one we were with the majority of the time. That way we could stay at our private middle and high schools that he was paying for. We saw my mom every other day until she moved to Michigan; now we see her twice a year. I always felt awkward about the divorce because I didn't quite understand what was going on, and my parents' relationship had become so overwhelmed with the differences of time that they seemed more like roommates than lovers.

When the divorce first happened, it wasn't as traumatizing as most people assumed it would be for me. I still had two parents in my life. Yeah, one was more involved than the other, but I still had them both. I got two Christmases each year, two bedrooms that I got to decorate; my life was mostly still intact. I was also ten at the time, so I was more absorbed with my American Girl dolls and my life-size toy car that I could drive around the front yard. I was thinking about seeing my mom and David again when my thoughts were interrupted by Marissa.

"Alright sweetie, everything looks good. I will leave this clipboard at the bottom of your bed for any other nurses that come in," she said as she walked to the foot of my bed. "It's about ten thirty, so I recommend you try to get some rest. Your therapist will be by late tomorrow morning to introduce herself and get to know you a little better. If you need to use the restroom or you aren't feeling well during the night, don't forget you can just click the button next to you. You are not allowed to use the restroom alone or walk anywhere alone yet, so just buzz me and I will take you where you would like to go!"

I nodded my head and smiled.

"Goodnight, Adelynn, sleep well!" she said as she put down the clipboard and left the room.

_____

CHAPTER TWO

Adjusting

ROLLED OVER, FACING the window that had a view of the city. I looked at the skyline, tracing the tips of the skyscrapers with my eyes. I love the lights of the city, and the long, narrow streets. There is always something to do and somewhere to be, but the city doesn't rush you. You can indulge in the moment wherever you are standing. My favorite part of the city is Central Park. It's a long park, but it's a great one. It's nice to walk around there and get lost for a few hours. My favorite thing to do in the park is to sit and paint; just set up my easel in one place and fill the canvas. I'll paint the people that walk by me or paint the trees. Paint the walkways or paint the horses that roam throughout the park. Every single time I've brought my paint supplies to that park, I've walked out with a gorgeous picture. Art can be hard sometimes, and sometimes I get dissatisfied with it, but every painting I have made within that park has come out immaculate.

Occasionally, I will bring a book and sit below the trees in Central Park and read. Among my favorite books are *Pride and Prejudice*, *Beautiful Disaster*, *Call Me by Your Name*, and really any other adult romance novel. I purchased each of those particular books at a bookstore on Broadway and then took a taxi to the park to begin my adventure. I am unsure if I like creating art better than reading. Reading is nice because I can enter someone else's world, but art is nice because I can show someone else mine.

I can't imagine I will get too much sleep tonight, if any. I mean after all, I have been sleeping for a week straight. I rolled over and sat up. The TV remote was next to my bed, so I picked it up and turned on the TV. ABC7 was already on, so I put the remote on my lap, adjusted my bed with the button, sat straight up and watched the news. The first story: "NYPD battle ongoing violence, gang war in NYC as Cuomo, Adams meet to discuss violence." Andrew Cuomo and Eric Adams met up to discuss the violence on Tuesday. A twenty-five-year-old was shot in the head just after midnight on Tuesday morning, two days after a thirteen-year-old was shot in the head. That is the one thing I was always taught about New York City: don't let the shine of the skyline fool you after sundown because once the sun sets, the gangs come out.

"Laundromat employee punched, hit in the head with a vase in Brooklyn." "Search on for gunman who tried to rob Dior on Fifth Avenue." "Eighteen-year-old injured in a random attack with a fishing hook beside a lake." "Man suffers burns in random liquid attack on NYC sidewalk." "Hungry trespassers break into a popular NYC dumpling restaurant." The news is making the city I love sound bad, but there's stories like "Goats race through Manhattan's Riverside Park as the weed-whacking herd returns." Okay, maybe that doesn't make the city sound better, but it really is a great city during the day, and it's nice to admire, from a distance, at night. I was just about done watching the news. If anything *that* important happens, then I'm sure I will hear about it eventually. I clicked the guide button and put on a random show.

I watched a few episodes until I got hungry. It's one in the morning and I feel bad for ringing Marissa, but I'm not sure where the cafeteria is, and I'm not allowed to walk alone. I shut off the TV and clicked the red button to call Marissa. It lit up and then began blinking. A few minutes later Marissa walked in the door, clicked the button attached to her waistband, and my button shut off. She walked to the foot of my bed, sat down, and looked at me.

"Hello again Adelynn, are you okay? What do you need?"

"I'd like to go to the cafeteria. Is it open?"

"Yes! It's open 24/7!"

Marissa took the blanket off my body and adjusted my legs so they dangled over the side of the bed. She grabbed my hand and helped pull me up so I was standing upright. She held my hands and walked backward while leading me out the door of the hospital room. I began walking by slowly putting one foot in front of the other, just really focusing on my steps. It felt like it took forever to get into the hallway, but once I did she had a walker ready for me. She placed my hands on the handles and stood by my side. With every step I took, I would shift the walker forward slightly with my arms so I could move more easily. It took a while to get to the elevator, but when we did, Marissa clicked the up button. She held the door open while I worked my way inside. Once I was in she entered and clicked the button for the twenty-fifth floor. As the elevator began to move, she helped me turn around so I was facing the doors once more, and she held the doors open (again) when we got to our floor as I worked my way out. A sign on the wall across from us indicated the cafeteria was to the right. I slowly shuffled in that direction and Marissa followed.

The cafeteria was at the end of a long hallway, straight down from the elevator. I worked my way over to the closest table. Marissa helped me sit down and pulled a bottle of hand sanitizer off her belt. I put out my hands for a squirt. While I began rubbing my hands together to spread the sanitizer, she stood across from me at the other end of the table.

"Okay love, I will get you something to eat. What would you like?" she asked me.

"Can I maybe get some ice cream? I'm sure that feeding tube liquid tasted disgusting; I'd like to give my body some actual good food," I said, smirking. I fiddled with the necklace around my neck.

"Well, I'm technically not supposed to, but if you eat some fruit before the ice cream, I'll let you have it. What is your favorite kind of fruit?" she asked.

"Watermelon," I answered.

"I like watermelon too. What kind of ice cream would you like?"

"Vanilla," I told her.

"I'll be back!" she exclaimed as she smiled and turned away.

Marissa returned with a bowl of freshly cut watermelon. She placed the bowl in front of me and handed me a fork. My hands were still shaky; actually, my whole body was still shaky. I speared a piece of watermelon while Marissa sat down across from me.

"So, Adelynn, why don't you tell me a little about yourself?"

"Well, I am eighteen years old, I am from Long Island, I like to paint and I also like to read. I have two sisters and both of my parents have remarried after a divorce. I am just about to graduate high school and I have already begun the college search process. I have it narrowed down to five schools. I will be visiting each of them within the next few months," I told her.

"That is quite awesome! What schools are you considering?"

"New York University, Merrimack College, Southern New Hampshire University, Central Michigan University, and the School of the Art Institute of Chicago."

"Well those are quite good options, that's a very big decision!"

"Yeah it definitely is; it's kinda intimidating."

"Well, I'm sure you will be just fine. What is your main school choice as of right now?"

"The School of the Art Institute of Chicago. From the research I've done so far, I think that could really be the best place for me."

"That's very good! What do your parents think? Do they have any college choices they prefer?"

"Well, my father really likes New York University because he went there. My mother likes Central Michigan University because it is closer to her. My sister goes to Southern New Hampshire University so she is encouraging me to go there."

"Wow; that definitely could make a big impact on your decision. I'm sure wherever you go, you will do wonderfully," she said as she smiled.

Just as I was finishing up my watermelon, Marissa got up to get me my ice cream. While she was gone, I looked around the hospital cafeteria. The cafeteria here was quite nice. It had bright white and blue flooring with white walls and blue trim. All of the tables were round, surrounded by chairs. On the walls were multiple posters that reminded people to wash their hands or use sanitizer, or emphasized having a healthy diet. The digital clock above the large double doors leading in and out of the cafeteria read 3:32 AM. The area the food was served was buffet style. Sure, most of the cafeteria was closed because of the time of day, but one chef was behind the counter waiting to make someone a midnight snack. The ceiling was tiled but had large circular windows where light could make its way through during the day. I was able to look up at the stars through these circles. The light in the cafeteria was minimal because only four lights in the corners of the room kept it lit at night.

There was one other patient in the cafeteria, but they had their back turned towards me so I could not make out much of their face. I did notice they were eating a small bowl of pasta with red sauce and had on a standard hospital gown. He was sitting alone and eating with his head down. He had broad shoulders and short dark hair. I assumed he must be no older than nineteen.

Marissa returned with a massive sugar cone topped with perfectly swirled soft-serve vanilla ice cream. I smiled as I took the cone from her and she sat down at my table once more. In her other hand, Marissa had tiny plastic bags with a variety of toppings for my ice cream. She placed them on the table in front of me and smiled. There were rainbow sprinkles, chocolate sprinkles, M&Ms, and Oreos.

"They didn't have much of a selection for toppings back there, but I figured I would grab you some just in case you wanted to spice up your ice cream a little bit."

"Thank you, Marissa!"

I held the ice cream in my right hand and picked out the M&Ms to put on top of it. I sprinkled on the candy and, to my surprise, I got every M&M on the ice cream without dropping a single one. I was eating my treat when Marissa started another conversation with me.

"What are you planning on majoring in at college? Do you know what career path you would like to take?" she asked.

"Well, if I go to SAIC then I will probably major in what they call New Arts Journalism and minor in Art Design and Politics."

"That's amazing! Do you have any specific reason for selecting that major and minor?"

"I really enjoy reading and art and both of those hobbies are combined in the major I am hoping to have. As far as my minor goes, I like reading about historical events and politics, so I think that having a minor that includes art *and* politics will be a nice fit for me."

"It's definitely good that you know what you like and you can apply that to your future! I'm excited for you! I'm sure once you get out of here you won't want to look back, but you should definitely stay in touch once you start college!"

"Wow, thank you, that's so sweet of you! How did you become a nurse? What made you want to do it?"

"My grandfather passed away when I was very young. I remember seeing him at the hospital and I had an urge to help others. I wanted to be a pharmacist originally because I wasn't sure if the hospital environment was right for me, but after taking some pharmaceutical classes, I knew *that* wasn't the right environment for me, so I tried the nursing program at my local college. By the end of my first semester, I loved it and knew this was what I wanted to do as a career," she told me.

"That is really an inspiring story. I'm sorry about you grandfather;

that must have been quite hard. I'm really inspired by the way you turned things that weren't so great into something special that helps people."

In the middle of Marissa thanking me, the boy that was sitting at the other table walked past ours. He had thrown his bowl away and was headed towards the cafeteria doors. Marissa turned towards him and began speaking to him.

"Hey buddy, are you going back up to your room?"

The boy paused and looked at Marissa. "Yes," he responded.

I looked at his face and was immediately intrigued. He had light blue eyes with dark hair and a structured face. Marissa wished him a goodnight and he smiled at her. He had a nice, soft smile. He exited the room and Marissa looked back at me. I guess she caught me staring a little too long.

"Adelynn?" she said while leaning in a little closer to see if I was zoned out.

"Yes?" I asked while making eye contact with her.

"Sorry for cutting off our last conversation but that's Zac. I just wanted to make sure he knew where he was going. He is on the same floor as you so he's also one of my patients. He should be out of here soon though."

"What is he here for?"

"I'm technically not supposed to disclose why he's here, but he had a fishing accident and had to get stitches across his stomach. He's been here for about a week now and his stomach is finally starting to heal."

"Well that's good."

Marissa could tell I was more intrigued by this boy than I was letting on. I went back to eating my ice cream and Marissa continued talking with me.

"So Adelynn, do you have any pets?"

"Yes," I said, "I have a dog named Charli at home. She's a little white bull terrier. You know the little white puppies that always have round faces and usually have pointed noses?"

"Yes! My grandmother has one of those!"

I laughed. "That's awesome! I also have a pet hamster named Mr. Whiskers." I paused, looked down and smiled. "I named him when I was fifteen, or else he would have a different name," I chuckled.

"Mr. Whiskers is a great name," Marissa said, giggling.

"Yeah for the pet of a three-year-old," I laughed.

I continued eating my ice cream and finished the cone. Marissa brought the bags of toppings that I didn't use back up to the chef and then returned back to me.

"Are you ready to head back downstairs, Adelynn?"

"Yes, can we just stop at the restroom first?"

"Absolutely."

Marissa took my hands and guided them to the walker beside the table. She stood by my side as we exited the cafeteria and started back down the hall. We walked straight down the hallway, all the way past the elevators, and Marissa helped me into the women's room. Marissa walked out of the bathroom and into the hall to wait for me. The bathroom had three stalls. The tiles on the walls were pink and the floor had little baby pink tiles. I used the restroom and wobbled over to the sink to wash my hands. There were three sinks with a mirror in front of each one. I stepped in front of the middle sink and pushed the soap dispenser so I could wash my hands. I turned on the water and began rubbing my hands together.

I looked up at the mirror and saw myself for the first time since I woke up in the hospital. My long dark brown hair was slightly messy. My freckles looked quite defined in the dim bathroom light. I looked a little closer and saw that my hazel eyes were green tonight. My cheeks were really red and my rosacea was pretty bad. I finished washing my hands and grabbed two pieces of paper towel. I wiped my hands, threw the paper towel away and turned towards the walker. I grabbed the handles and worked my way out of the bathroom.

Marissa brought me back over to the elevator and clicked the down button. We got into the elevator and she clicked the button for the eighth floor. The elevator brought me back to my floor and Marissa helped me get back to my room. She helped me into my bed and asked if I needed anything more. I shook my head and she left. I turned on my TV again and flipped through the stations until I found something to watch.

CHAPTER THREE

———

Exploring

I SAT IN FRONT of my TV for hours. The sun came up around eight. Two hours later, a woman with long black hair and green eyes walked into my room. She was dressed in purple scrubs that had a flower design. She padded to the foot of my bed and picked up the clipboard. I reached for the remote and muted my TV. She examined the clipboard and slowly walked to the head of the bed. Arriving at my right, she stood and looked up at me.

"Good morning Adelynn! My name is Crystal and I'm your primary nurse! Have you met Marissa already?"

"Yes, I have! It is nice to meet you, Crystal!"

"It's nice to meet you too! I have some routine questions I have to ask you, and some introductory questions and topics that we have to talk about! Do you feel comfortable doing this now?"

"Yes, uhm, that sounds great to me!" I gripped the armrests of the bed to push my lower body out of its slouch, my head facing Crystal as I moved.

"Alright let's begin. How are you feeling? I see that you woke up for good about twelve hours ago!"

"I'm feeling alright. I'm still pretty shaken. I haven't done much walking and it is hard when I do. I've been using a walker."

"I see. It says here that you are on antidepressants. Zoloft?"

"Yes, thirty milligrams."

"And you take those every night, correct?"

"Yes, every night before bed."

"Alright. Due to you being on a feeding tube while you were comatose, we are going to slowly ease your body back into taking the prescription. We discussed this with your primary care doctor and they recommended you take ten milligrams each night for the next week, twenty each night the following week, and then we can return you to your original dosage. It also says here that you will be meeting with a therapist to ensure that the physical suffering your head endured doesn't cause any other mental health concerns. Are you comfortable with this?"

"Yes."

"Okay, I am going to put you on a pill that should help ease any pain you are having. You must take the pill once a day, so you can just take it along with your Zoloft at night."

"Okay."

"Additionally, your therapist's name is Joyce and she will be coming in around noon today."

"Okay, thank you."

"It also says here that your father put five people on the list to come visit you. Because you are eighteen, we can make adjustments to this list however you would like. That was just a temporary fix because of your coma. On the list we have William Davis, Elizabeth Davis, Victoria Davis, Harper Scott, and Andrew Scott. Would you like to make any changes to this list?"

I guess that answers my question of why my mom or David didn't come to see me. Of course, my father only put his side of the family.

"Yes, I would like to change some things."

"Alright, if you could just provide me with the first and last names of the people you would like on this list as well as their addresses, emails, their relationship to you, and their phone numbers. You can have a list of up to ten people."

"Thank you! The people on the list already can stay. Do you need any information for them or are they all set?"

"Your father provided us with all that information so you are all set with those people. Who would you like to add?"

"I would like to add my mom. Her name is Claire Davis. Her address is 10 Badger Court in Farwell, Michigan. Her email is ccarter359@eyereminds.com. Her phone number is 989-298-4561. I would also like to add my stepfather David Carter. His address is the same as my mom's and his email is dcarter982@eyereminds.com. His phone number is 989-298-4567."

"Thank you, Adelynn. Is there anyone else you would like to add?"

This question didn't require much thinking. I was contemplating adding my grandparents on my dad's side, but the chances of them visiting were slim. I wouldn't want them to come anyway. They have had extremely long and hard lives. My grandfather fought in World War II. He was drafted when he had just turned eighteen. My grandmother met him right before that. She had a hard time mentally while he was away and when he came back to visit she fell while pregnant. She lost the baby a few months later. This wouldn't be their first miscarriage; actually, they had multiple. My father was the only child my grandparents had and he was their last attempt at having a baby. They were both forty when my dad was born. They raised him and sent him to college and he moved out on his own where he then met my mom.

My grandfather was diagnosed with fibromyalgia about five years ago and is also slowly losing his eyesight and hearing. They finally just settled into Florida a few years ago and I see them every year at Christmas. Christmas is only a few weeks away and I'm sure by then this will all be a funny memory.

I could add my one best friend at school, but I'm sure my father has been keeping in touch with her mother and I don't want her to see me like this. However, I guess I could use the company.

"Yes, just one more person. Peyton Hayes. She is my best friend. Her phone number is 613-495-3918. Her email is phayes082503@ remindmail.com. Her address is 333 Park Ave, New York, New York. It's apartment 2D."

"Alright, and is she also eighteen?"

"Yes."

"Okay. I added them to the list so they are all set. Would you like us to get in contact with them?"

"Yes please."

"Alright. Is the best way to contact them via phone?"

"For everyone besides my mom, yes. Contact her via email."

"Sounds good. I'm sure you have been wondering where your phone is. We took it while you were in your coma. That way no one else could get ahold of it and your private information could stay secure."

"Thank you. I appreciate that."

"You can get your phone back whenever you would like."

"Thank you. I honestly don't mind not having it so maybe in a few days."

"That's good. I honestly admire that. Not many girls your age have that response. Usually, they wake up and their phone is the first thing they ask for."

I chuckled. "I barely use my phone anyways. It isn't the end of the world."

"Alright, well just let us know when you would like it."

"Thank you."

"So now we can move to more general questions. What clothes make you feel the most comfortable? You won't have to wear a hospital gown here all the time; in fact since you are feeling better we can get you some clothes to wear today. The hospital has its own closet of clean clothes that we can provide to our patients, and you can also have your family bring you some clothes as well."

"That sounds good. My style is more comfortable rather than fashionable. I usually wear sweatpants."

"Well, we can get those for you for sure. What size are you?"

"Small."

"Perfect. So what is your typical schedule like? What times do you usually eat throughout the day?"

"I usually eat breakfast when I wake up around nine. I eat lunch at twelve thirty and dinner at about seven thirty. I usually try to eat a healthy snack in the afternoon at about four."

"Would you like to keep that schedule while you are here?"

"Yes, I think that will probably be the best for me."

"Alright, so each day I will come up to get you at those times and help you get to the cafeteria. If you get hungry at a different time or want to change your schedule you can just let me know."

"Thank you."

"Of course. Now let's talk about school. We've stayed in contact with your principal, and your teachers have been quite helpful and understanding. They are leaving the choice up to you. They have been compiling folders of work for you that you can complete whenever you are ready and you have extended deadlines. You can do the work here, or you can wait until you are discharged to do the work. Whatever you feel most comfortable doing."

"I think I want to do the work here and begin to catch up."

"Alright, we will let your school know, and we will make arrangements with your teachers to get the work for you. Most of your teachers have offered to drop the work off here because your school is so close to this hospital." She paused and ran her eyes from the top of the clipboard to the bottom, making sure she didn't miss anything. "Alright, so that's enough questioning you for now. Do you want to take a shower?"

"Yes please."

"Okay. I'm gonna head downstairs to get you an outfit you can wear after we get you washed up and make sure there's an available shower room."

"Thank you."

Crystal finished making notes on the clipboard and walked back towards the door. She left the room, and I lay back down, placing my head on my pillow. I unmuted the TV and continued watching my show. About twenty minutes later, Crystal reentered the room with a pair of gray, folded sweatpants and a large-size plain white t-shirt. I shut off the TV as she placed the clothes on my bed. She unfolded the shirt and held it up.

"So, the only shirt I could find was this large t-shirt. Is this alright with you?"

"Yes, that is fine. It looks comfortable. Thank you!"

"Alright. I have a walker for you out in the hallway if you need it. There's shampoo and conditioner in the shower room, as well as a bar of soap and a few towels. We have a selection of undergarments in there and you can pick what feels most comfortable once you shower. When you shower, if you need anything there is a button on the wall. It's for an intercom; you can tell us what the problem is while you're showering and we can assess the best way to help you. Privacy is our main concern, especially when you are in the shower room."

"Thank you!"

"Alright, let's get you to the shower!"

Crystal helped me up and out of bed. My body was still a little shaky. I could not walk on my own without the walker, so Crystal helped me get to it and aided me as I push-stepped down the hall. Crystal carried the clothes for me and clicked the up button on the elevator. We got in the elevator and she hit the button for the next floor up. We were quickly brought up to the ninth floor. We turned to our left and there were five different doors, each labeled "Shower Room." We walked over to "Shower Room 4" and Crystal unlocked the door. I left the walker in the hallway and she handed me the clothes.

I walked through the door and was in the shower room. The light was on, as well as a fan to help with ventilation. There was a large mirror on the wall and a bench below the mirror. I placed the clothes on the bench and walked over to the shower. I turned on the shower by pulling the knob and then began to undress. I took my shower and when I got out I wrapped the towel around me. I opened the door and pulled my walker from the hallway to walk over to the bench and saw a selection of undergarments; they were in a dispenser-type machine, hanging on the wall next to the mirror. I selected the ones I wanted and, as I got dressed, took a longer look around the shower room. The room was painted white halfway from the ceiling down; the other half was completely tiled. The tiles were a brown marble color that continued to the tiled floor. When I was done, I felt much, much better. Sometimes I underestimate the power of a warm shower and clean clothes.

I left the bathroom with my towel and dirty hospital gown in hand. Crystal was down the hall, talking to another nurse. She saw that I was done and came towards me, putting out her hand so she could take the dirty clothes. I handed her the clothes and shut the shower room door behind me.

"How was it? Do you feel better now?"

"Yes, very!" I responded.

"Good, good. While you were in the shower, I placed your Zoloft and your pain medicine on your night table. The bottle that says hydromorphone is the one that will be helping you with your night pain."

"Perfect, thank you."

"You should start taking them tonight. You also have a different, nondrowsy pain med for any pain during daylight hours, but you definitely don't want to take any medications on an empty stomach! Would you like to head to the cafeteria and get some food now?"

"Yes please, I'm starving."

"Alright. Do you think you can walk without the walker?"

"Uhmmm...I think so. I mean I'm going to have to get back to walking without it eventually."

"Alright. Let's get you upstairs!"

We began walking down the hallway without the walker. I could barely feel my legs and it was obvious they were shaking badly. So naturally, I soon stumbled and fell to the ground. Crystal helped me up and had me lean against a wall while she went back into the shower room to grab my walker. Once she returned with it, Crystal and I got upstairs to the cafeteria. Quite disappointed that I was still having trouble walking, I looked up and noticed the cafeteria was completely full. Almost every table was occupied by at least one patient. I told Crystal I was going to get some food and she went over to some other tables to greet her coworkers or other patients that she was a nurse for. On my plate, I got eggs, a little bit of bacon, and some fruit. I wanted to keep it somewhat light for breakfast to make sure my stomach could handle normal food. I found an empty table at the back of the cafeteria, sat down, and began eating.

About halfway through my meal, I felt a presence, a shadow standing over me. I looked up from my plate and I saw a boy standing on the other side of the table. My eyes met his. He had light green eyes with specks of brown throughout. The world seemed to stop for a moment. My peripheral vision blurred until he was the only thing I could see. My hearing slowly began to fade, until he opened his mouth to speak.

"Hi," he said to me.

"Hey," I responded.

"Is it cool if I sit here?" He paused. "The cafeteria is kinda full, or, well I know you know it's full because you can see that. Or at least I'm assuming you can. Anyways, I need a place to sit. Can I sit with you?"

I giggled a little bit. "Yeah," I said to him, "of course."

He placed his plate down on the table and sat down across from me.

"I'm Lucas," he said as he picked up his fork.

"I'm Adelynn."

I looked back down at my plate and began eating my eggs. Lucas began eating as well. He had a plate with an omelet, a side of hash browns, and two pieces of bacon. He was cutting into his omelet when he looked up at me and started a conversation.

"So uhm, how long have you been here for?"

"I've been here for just about a week I guess. How about you?"

"I've been here for about two weeks."

"Really? What got you in here?"

"I tore my ACL while playing football."

"Wow, I'm sorry. That must be awful. Where do you go to school?"

"I just graduated from Stonington High School last year and now I'm a wide receiver for the New York University football team."

"Wow, New York University is really expensive right?"

"Yeah, which could definitely be a problem for me. They are considering taking away my scholarship money if I don't get better in time."

"For real? That's so awful. How could they do that?"

"Well I don't know if you know much about NYU, but its football team is Division I, meaning we are the best of the best when it comes to college football. They need a good wide receiver to keep that going and if I can't play they want to give that scholarship money to someone else that can."

"I didn't even know they could do that."

"They can and they will, unfortunately."

"That's awful. I'm so sorry."

The conversation died out for a moment. I was still mind-blown at the fact that they can take away a scholarship so quickly. New York University was on my list of potential schools, but maybe it shouldn't be after all. I wasn't planning on playing any sports, but that still just doesn't seem right to me. I know how stressful college searching can be. After doing all that hard work to get into such a pristine school, to finally get there and begin playing, just to tear a ligament and have all that go down the drain in a matter of seconds, shocked me. NYU has a 16 percent acceptance rate and it's not like it's a cheap college. It's $75,000 before any financial aid is applied, and the lowest amount possible based on household income is still a good $30,000.

With my dad always working at a well-paying job and us living on Long Island you may assume my financial situation isn't too bad, which it isn't. I was luckily born into a family on the wealthier side, but I want to pay for college myself. Take out loans and earn the education, and then earn the money to pay for said education. I don't want to owe my family—more specifically my dad and Elizabeth—anything, so I'll be paying all by myself. I began fiddling with my necklace.

"I had NYU on my list of potential colleges," I told him. "I mean I don't know how I feel now. I didn't know that they could just take money away like that."

"Well, I don't want to scare you. Would you be playing any sort of sport if you did go to NYU?"

"Well, no."

"Then don't worry. You should be perfectly fine if you just keep your grades up. I don't know your specific financial information—I mean duh, obviously I don't—but regardless, if you get a good academic scholarship and you keep your GPA up you should be perfectly fine. Where do you go to school now?"

"I go to Newcomers High School. It's right down the street from here."

"Wow, I have met a lot of people that went there and they all said it was a great school. How do you like it there?"

"Well, it's alright I guess. All of the teachers are nice."

"That's good!"

"Yeah." I paused. I felt quite unsure of what to say to him. I couldn't get the thought of him losing his scholarship out of my mind. Here I am, feeling bad for someone that I just met not even five minutes ago. I was still staring at my plate when I caught him looking up at me from the corner of my eye. I looked up and he smiled. I like his smile; it's gentle and kind. I don't know how he can sit here and smile at me right now. If I was in his position I'm sure I would be a frantic, nervous mess. I smiled back at him and giggled a tiny little bit. I had the urge to know more about him, but I didn't know why.

"So, you went to Stonington High School right?" I asked.

"Yes," he answered.

"Where is that?"

"It's in Stonington, Connecticut."

"I've never heard of it. How far is that from here?"

"It's about three hours away."

"That's a pretty good distance."

"Yeah, for sure." The conversation died out again, but he picked it back up quickly. "Well, now that I have told you about me, why don't you tell me about yourself? What are you doing in this place?"

"I'm still not entirely sure. I was told I was in a car accident that resulted in me falling into a coma for a week. I just woke up last night."

"Oh my god! Were you alone in the car?"

"I honestly don't know. I never got answers about anything. All I remember is going to bed last Thursday night. I don't know where I was, who I was with, or how I got here. All I know is I woke up last night and here I am."

"That does not sound good at all. How are you feeling now?"

"I have to use a walker for a little bit to get around but I'm doing okay."

"That's good. I'm glad you're okay. A coma is a serious thing."

"Yeah. I'm sure I'll be okay." I looked up at the clock, which boldly declared the time as 11:16 AM. Good thing I had just finished my food. Joyce would be at my room to talk to me soon and Elizabeth was supposed to be coming sometime this morning. I picked up my napkin and plastic fork and piled everything on my plate.

"You leaving?" Lucas asked.

"Yeah, I should probably get going. I have an appointment I have to get to."

"Alright," he responded. "Well thank you so much for letting me sit with you. It was nice talking to you."

"It was nice meeting you too!" I looked at Lucas and smiled. I got up out of my chair and picked up my food.

"Goodbye Lucas."

"Goodbye Adelynn."

I used my walker to make my way to the trash and throw away my plate. I looked around and saw Crystal talking to one of her coworkers. I didn't want to bother her and already knew where I was going, so I turned myself and my walker towards the cafeteria doors and left. When I got back up to my room, it was empty. Elizabeth wasn't there and Joyce wasn't coming for another forty-five minutes, so I sat on my bed and turned on my TV. I flipped through the stations until I found something that could keep me entertained.

About twenty minutes later, Crystal came in to give me water for my daylight pain meds. I noticed the bottle was labeled "Naproxen Sodium," and that's when she began telling me about side effects.

CHAPTER FOUR

Vulnerability

"ALRIGHT, SO YOUR father mentioned you don't have any allergies, so if you get any weird symptoms like itching, extreme drowsiness, or lightheadedness, just use the button."

She gave me some water, gave me my pill, and left.

When noon rolled around, Joyce came to my door. She had long auburn hair that was pulled back into a high ponytail and she was dressed very professionally. She had a clipboard in her hand that she placed on the chair under the board on the wall. She pulled the chair over to the end of my bed, grabbed her clipboard off the chair seat, and sat down while I turned off my TV.

"Hello Adelynn, my name is Joyce and I am your new hospital therapist. I already spoke to your father and he gave me some background information about you. I have a clipboard here with that and all of your other information. I would like to run through everything with you and then we can get started with our session!"

"Alright!"

"So you are on a thirty milligram dose of Zoloft?"

"Yes."

"And Marissa or Crystal already talked to you about easing you back into your normal dosage?"

"Yes, Crystal and I talked about it."

"Perfect. And you are on Zoloft to treat your depression?"

"Yes."

"Alright, and have you seen a therapist before, or are you seeing one besides me?"

"No."

"Okay, well I did just want to let you know that anything that you tell me here is completely confidential. I only have to report a situation if it has the potential to cause serious physical harm to yourself or others. Everything else that we talk about here stays between you and me."

"Okay."

"So because of this, I am going to ask you to be honest about everything. If there is a question you feel uncomfortable answering, you can just tell me. Feel free to be as descriptive as you would like in your answers and if I need clarification on something I will ask."

"That sounds good to me."

"Alright, so since therapy is a new thing for you, I want to take a minute to ask you about the relationships in your life so I can get a feel for what the dynamics of our therapeutic relationship may be like. Can you tell me about some of the important relationships in your life?"

"Well, I would have to say my most important relationships are with my mom, Peyton, who is my best friend from school, and my oldest sister Harper."

"It's good that you have a couple of people on this list. Is there anything you would like me to know about your family? Your father mentioned that your parents are divorced. How does this make you feel?"

"Well, it doesn't affect me as one might think it does. I mean sometimes it can make things uncomfortable but it isn't that bad."

"What was it like growing up in your family?"

"It was alright. It was uncomfortable a lot of the time because my mom was there and my dad wasn't and they seemed more like roommates. When my mom moved out, my father met someone new and continued his work habits so he was never around, and I don't have a close relationship with my stepmom. Whenever I'm home now, I just spend time alone in my room doing homework, watching TV, writing, or drawing."

"Could you list some wrongs that have been done to you by others that you haven't forgotten, no matter how long it's been?"

"I don't have any. I mean, my first ever boyfriend cheated on me my freshman year and obviously that sucked, but I have gotten over it."

"Wow, I'm sorry to hear that. What happened?"

"Well we dated for six months and I walked in on him with another girl."

"And how did you react to this?"

"I left."

"Can you elaborate a little more?"

"Well, when I caught him with her it was clear that he was no longer someone I could trust. So I just left. I blocked him and never spoke to him again." I fiddled with my necklace.

"Wow, I've never heard that answer before. That is incredibly brave and strong of you!"

"I mean he did try to get back with me for weeks. He made school torture for me. He'd follow me around and stuff but once my peers started catching on they put a stop to that. Word about him cheating on me spread like wildfire."

"Well it is good they supported you. What do you think caused you to be treated for depression? Is there any particular event that may have triggered the depression?"

"I don't think so. As I started going through grade school I just started getting sadder and sadder. Eventually, I told my mom how I was feeling and she told my doctor and we got Zoloft prescribed to me."

"And how long ago was this?"

"When my mom was still living in New York, probably about four years ago."

"Okay, can you describe your typical daily mood for me? Is it more like a roller coaster or is it pretty steady?"

"I would say my mood is pretty steady."

"Alright, that's good. What is something that makes you feel more upbeat and happy?"

"I would probably say drawing or reading."

"That's very good! Are those some of your favorite hobbies?"

"Yes."

"Good, good. When you get upset, what are some ways that you take out your frustrations? "

"I mean it depends on the situation. If I'm at school and I get frustrated by a classmate then I will probably just put in earbuds and listen to music or go to the art wing if I can. If I'm at home and my family upsets me, chances are I'll just go to my room and read or draw. If I am at my mom's house and this happens, she will normally come talk to me about what upset me, but if I'm at my father's house, I'll usually just use my hobbies to calm myself down."

"Okay. Some people use drugs, alcohol, caffeine, or other coping methods to make themselves feel better. Do you find yourself using any of these to cope?"

"Not often."

"Alright. How often would you say you use one or more of these methods to cope?"

"Very rarely."

"Is it a last resort type thing for you?"

"Yeah, my day has got to be pretty bad if I turn to that."

"When you do, is it drugs, alcohol, caffeine, or something else?"

"Alcohol. I don't smoke."

"Alright. So, when you feel like you need to talk to someone about your feelings or moods, who do you usually go to?"

"I rarely talk to anyone about my emotions, but if I do it's Peyton or my mom."

"What about Harper?"

"Well, because she has a kid now and a life of her own I just let her do her thing. I've got two people and that is plenty of support."

"So how do you talk to your mom about what is bothering you? Do you call her?"

"I usually email her; she doesn't like talking on the phone."

"Alright. Have you dated anyone since your ex?"

"No."

"Is it because you haven't had the opportunity or because you don't want to?"

"Well at first I wanted to move on to someone new, but the girl he cheated on me with made that simply impossible."

"Who is she?"

"Well, she's the popular cheerleader that everyone loves. After he stopped chasing me because of the other people in my class, he started dating her for good. Her name is Nevaeh. She and Alec will be celebrating their third anniversary this upcoming May."

"And Alec is your ex-boyfriend?"

"Yes."

"How exactly did she make dating impossible for you? She got Alec so why did she attack you?"

"She just didn't like me. She would find out I was talking to some-one and she would text them and make them try to fall for her, then once I'd find out and move on she would ghost them and move on to whoever I was interested in next. Eventually, I just gave up."

"Okay." Joyce was writing down all of this information as I spoke. She scanned over the clipboard one more time to check and make sure there were no questions she had missed, and then she looked up at me.

"Alright well, we got every question on here completed so now I have all the information I need for us to begin regular sessions. It's just about half past twelve now and I know this is your scheduled lunchtime, so unless you have any questions or anything you would like to talk about I will let you go eat. Do you have anything else you would like to mention?"

"Nope, I think I'm all set for today."

"Perfect, I will talk to Crystal about your schedule and I will be back within a few days when you are available!" She stood up and put the chair back up against the wall before she headed to the door.

"Thank you, it was nice meeting you Joyce."

"It was nice meeting you too Adelynn, I'll see you soon!"

She left the room and shut the door behind her. I turned on my TV again; I wanted to get a little hungrier before I got food. Because of this, I didn't even end up getting lunch. I remained in my room watching TV until sometime after seven. I clicked the button to call Crystal and she brought me my walker to help me go to the cafeteria for dinner.

Got there, got in line, got my food: a large Caesar salad with chicken on top. The cafeteria was packed once again but the seats weren't as limited now. I found a table, sat down, and ate my dinner. When I was finished, I returned to my room and began watching TV again. At half past ten Marissa poked her head into my room.

"Hi, Adelynn. I just came to check up on you! How was your day?"

"My day was good. It was quite peaceful."

"I'm very glad to hear that! You met with Joyce today, right?"

"Yes."

"And how did your appointment go?"

"It went well! I like Joyce. She is nice."

"Good, I'm glad to hear that. I figured she would be a good fit for you. Did you eat today?"

"Yes."

Marissa walked over to the edge of my bed and picked up the clipboard. She flipped past the first page and grabbed the pen she had in the pocket of her scrubs. "Alright, and what did you eat today?"

"This morning I had eggs with some fruit and bacon. Tonight I had a Caesar salad with chicken."

She began writing on the clipboard. "Was that it?"

"Yes."

"Alright. Well, I just wanted to check in and let you know I'm here. Let me know if you need anything!"

"Thank you!"

Marissa put down the clipboard and left the room. I watched TV for another hour or so and then I finally began feeling tired, so I shut off my light and went to sleep.

CHAPTER FIVE

Stargazing

THE DOOR OPENED and he stepped foot into my hospital room. He was a boy I had never seen before. Black hair, green eyes, defined cheeks with peach-colored lips. His face was very well-structured with a very defined jawline. He was wearing all black clothes with three gold chains hanging from his neck. His left middle finger had a thick, gold ring at the base of it. He was tall, much taller than me. He walked over to the left side of my bed and put his ring hand on my cheek. Shivers went shooting down my spine when he picked up my right hand. I felt safe and comfortable in his presence. Without him saying anything, I knew what he wanted to do. I got up and out of my hospital bed. While still holding my hand, he led me out of the room. We ran down the hall. The hall was empty and the layout of the building felt different. He led me to the elevator and we went up to the top floor. The twenty-eighth floor. We stepped out of the elevator into the hallway.

When we got to the ladder at the end of the hallway we climbed up it. He climbed up the ladder before me and when he reached the top, he climbed through the hole in the ceiling. I followed him up the ladder and looked up. There he and I were. Standing on the top of the hospital rooftop. I looked at him and he made eye contact with me. With him holding my hand, we walked over to the solid concrete portion of the roof. The air was cold. I wasn't shivering, however. A slight breath of wind passed over us; I could feel the air brush my skin. I could feel it on my face, in my hair, wrapped around my right hand which was holding his, and I could feel when the crisp wind left. I looked up at him. Our eyes locked for a short moment until he turned his head towards the city. I followed the direction of his gaze and could once again see the New York City skyline, although it looked much brighter here than it did from my hospital window. The Chrysler Building was the first thing I noticed, standing tall as ever, with the crescent dome-shaped details towards the top, so famously recognized by nearly every New York spectator. The lights at the top were golden, piercing the dark sky behind it. I began to turn my head when I heard his voice for the first time. I stood there for a second, almost paralyzed. I tried processing what exactly he just said, analyzing the sound of his deep voice and the tone he was speaking in as I grabbed my necklace. My body relaxed once my brain caught up to it.

"Beautiful isn't it? I've been searching for something that matches its beauty for years but I was always unable to find anything, until I saw you." Smooth. What he said was smooth. Both his tone of voice and his compliment were smooth. Perfect, even. The first words he said to me were presented in a perfect way. None of this made sense. Who is this guy? Why are we at the top of the hospital building, and why is he talking to me in such a way? These unsettling questions are running through my mind, however, I don't feel uncomfortable at all. I turned towards him and responded.

"Thank you, it's gorgeous up here. It looks a lot different than it does from my hospital bed." I looked down and all at once I realized something amazing: I can walk. I mean I could walk before, but now I can walk without being shaky, feeling weak, or needing a walker. I let go of his hand and turned around. Soon I was twirling slightly and maneuvering my way around the rooftop freely. This is something I haven't been able to do in my last two days of conscious recovery, and something my body hasn't been able to do in nearly a week and a half. He joined me. He started moving with me. Us maneuvering around on the rooftop with the view of the pretty skyline. It was like a scene out of a movie. I could feel my feet below me in the comfortable hospital shoes moving swiftly and effortlessly. I twirled. My hair was floating in the crisp wind as we moved. My baggy t-shirt was moving with me, and so was he. He grabbed both of my hands. His bright green eyes would go from staring into my hazel ones, to darting elsewhere when I broke eye contact with him every few seconds.

It was clear he wanted to say something but didn't quite know what. It wasn't necessary for either of us to speak, however, because our body language was already speaking in paragraphs. He let go of my left hand and placed his on my lower back, pulling me in close. Our bodies moved in synchrony. We rocked back and forth until he pulled his hand from my back and raised my hand up to signal me into a spin. Even twirling twice, I could tell he was watching me the whole time. I released his hand and went over to the edge of the rooftop facing away from the city. The stars were vibrant in the night sky; the Big Dipper was easily visible. He walked towards me and saw me looking up at the stars. I could hear him crouching on the ground and settling flat out on his back. I joined him. I lay on my back, spreading out my body completely, stretching out my legs and relaxing my muscles. I didn't want to take my eyes off the stars. He was only a few inches from me and I could feel him looking at me, but not in an unsettling way. He was admiring me.

"Aries," he said.

"What?" I responded.

"You're an Aries. Your birthday is March twenty-eighth, so you're an Aries."

I paused. How did he know about my birthday? It wasn't on the whiteboard in my hospital room. Unlike most girls my age, I don't know anything about zodiac signs. I've been told I'm an Aries and I know my father is a Taurus and my mother is a Leo, but I never invested the time to discover what any of that means. It's not that I can't understand it; I just find it odd to trust that the stars control every human on this planet. The universe is so big. Billions and billions and billions of miles of stars, planets, galaxies, and space. Humans and our little Earth are not nearly significant enough to the universe as a whole for any of the constellations surrounding us to impact what exactly we do. At the end of the day, whatever we do in our daily lives, whoever we have in our lives, and whoever we care about and love, it's all so extremely insignificant. If I choose one decision over another or my neighbor chooses one decision over another, it has the same relevance to the universe: absolutely none. It doesn't matter in the grand scheme of the universe. If global warming takes over and our planet dies, or if our sun finally self-destructs, none of that matters in the grand scheme. I knew my thoughts were getting too philosophical and he was waiting for a response, so I reeled in my universe thoughts and came up with something more down-to-earth to say to him.

"I don't know anything about my Zodiac sign," I said.

"Well," he responded, "the Aries constellation is located in the Northern Hemisphere. The word 'Aries' means 'the ram' in Latin. Most people under your sign are said to be brave, powerful, direct, independent, strong, innocent, assertive, and fearless. Your ruling planet is the sun and your element is fire. The constellation consists of five stars, with the brightest being Alpha, Beta, and Gamma Arietis, and as a matter of fact, there it is."

He pointed up towards the sky, slightly to the right of us. Stars. All I saw were stars. I didn't know what the constellation looked like or which stars specifically made it up. I'd turned my head back towards him with a half-smirk on my face when he realized my confusion.

"Sorry," he said. He began pointing out each star specifically, talking me through it as he went. I don't know how he knew this stuff, but he was so enthusiastic about it. He was diving so deep into detail that he either clearly knew what he was talking about, or was good at creating stories. Every sentence out of his mouth was so extremely detailed. After going through each star, telling me more about what traits Aries tend to possess and how compatible they are with other signs, he stopped. He ran out of things to say, but I wasn't going to allow him to stop there. I barely knew anything about zodiac signs, but after seeing the way he talked about it, I wanted to learn. I looked back at him.

"What's your sign?" I asked

"I'm a Leo, August third," he responded.

"Where is that?"

"Well," he said, "it's in the Northern Hemisphere. Leos tend to be creative, passionate, generous, warm-hearted, and humorous."

"Which stars is it?"

He smiled, "Well, unfortunately we can't see it right now because of the time of year; it's usually seen here in the spring."

"Makes sense," I said. He talked about this for a while, continuing on about his star sign. I'd be lying if I said I didn't love every single minute of it. The conversation switched topics a few times. Eventually, we got to the meaning of life. It's a deep topic, I know, but I felt comfortable discussing such a deep thing with him.

"Honestly," he said, "I think the meaning of life is love."

"Care to elaborate?" I asked.

"Love is essentially what every person chases after. In one form or another, we all want to be loved. From birth, we require the love of our parents; in grade school we require the love of our peers; and eventually, we require the love of another that we want to grow old with."

"I've never thought about it like that. Do you believe in soul mates?"

"I do. Do you?"

"I think so." I grabbed my necklace again.

"What do you mean?"

"I think soul mates exist but only to an extent. I think that soul mates exist but it's rare for people to find their soul mates."

"That makes sense to me, but I think about it a little differently. I don't think about the probability of finding them, but instead what happens when you do find them. I believe that soul mates have to do with reincarnation. Love is the meaning of life, and we go through each reincarnated life trying to find our soul mate. Once we find our soul mate, we complete that life with our soul mate. Eventually, our physical bodies expire but our souls don't, so we enter into new bodies with a new chance to find our partner. Eventually, we begin a life and our soul mate crosses paths with us nearly immediately and they are our first love in that life. Whether they meet us in grade school or they're friends at birth because their mothers are best friends, they are each other's first love and they spend their entire life together. Once they pass, that's it. They reach heaven and they spend eternity together happily."

"I never thought about that. I mean that actually makes a lot of sense." It was interesting, this conversation. Never once have I talked to anyone about this. His ideas were deep and interesting. I appreciated that for sure. Surely, this was not typical. I haven't had much experience with boys—I mean I only dated one and I don't have many guy friends—but I know enough about boys to know that most boys don't open up about things like this.

We stared at the stars for a while without saying much. Thoughts of the conversation we had and the sound of his voice swirled in my head. Neither one of us had much to say. Switching the conversation back on after touching on such a deep subject wasn't something I could figure out how to do. The silence wasn't awkward so I decided against trying to figure out what to say next.

What felt like years went by. We saw a shooting star or two while laying down looking at the sky. He broke the silence by asking me to dance again. There was no music, just the sound of our shoes touching the roof. I had no sense of time. I didn't want to know what time it was. We were rocking back and forth. He had his right hand on my lower back and his left hand holding my right. My head was resting on his chest when the sun began to rise. I felt the warm sun touch my cheeks when he pulled away from me.

"I have to go now," he said.

"Go where?" I asked.

"Away. Just for a bit though." He picked up my left hand once more and looked down, "Adelynn, I will love you tomorrow."

That was the last thing I remember.

———

CHAPTER SIX

Small Talk

I WOKE UP IN a sweat, nearly jumping out of my own skin. My heart was racing and I began gasping for air as I sat up in the hospital bed. I was in my hospital room. The door was closed, and everything was normal. As far as I could see, there were no signs I ever left the room. I lay back down and rolled over in confusion. What *happened*?

I began recapping everything in my brain when I heard a faint chuckle from the base of my bed. Elizabeth was sitting in the chair under the TV, laughing at me. I rolled over, back onto my back, and sat up once again. I didn't notice her when I first woke up but she'd definitely noticed me. She had her dark hair curled, designer clothing, obnoxious leather boots, and a bunch of makeup on. She was staring off into her little pocket mirror, fixing her lipstick when I looked up at her.

"I was hoping the coma would make you a little more attentive, but you're still as oblivious as ever," she said.

"It's nice to see you again too, Elizabeth," I responded. For some reason, this is how Elizabeth has always been towards me. She always points out small things like how oblivious I can be from time to time. I figured she would drop the subtle insults considering the fact I got into an accident, but it's great to see that she is as nudgy as ever. I never had a problem with her; usually, I just let it roll off my back. Elizabeth has two children of her own that live with their biological father because she is too luxury oriented to raise them. Quite frankly, her insults never affect me because I can nearly guarantee my own dedication will take me farther in my life than my dad's money could ever take her.

I looked down at my hands, paused, and said, "You're one day late."

"I was planning on coming yesterday," she said, "but my nail artist had to move my appointment back by a few hours, meaning I had more time than anticipated, so I decided to have a pool day with my girlfriends and come to you today instead."

I should have anticipated that she would do something like this. She showed up to Victoria's Confirmation an hour and a half late a few years ago, she showed up late to my sixteenth birthday party, and she's done more than that. I don't think she intentionally means to be late, I just think she doesn't care enough to put in the effort to make sure she is on time. However, it's clear to me right now that she chose her prim and proper friends and a day at the pool over coming to visit me and making sure I'm alive. I have nothing more that I want to say to her right now.

It took a solid few minutes of me sitting up in my bed staring at the wall for her to realize I wasn't going to say anything else.

"Did they tell you what you were in here for?" she asked.

"They told me about the accident," I responded.

"The *accident*?" she asked, as her eyes widened slightly.

"Uh, the car accident?" I said.

"Oh, yes, the car accident."

I gave her a bizarre stare. Why is she saying it like that? I'm getting the sense that there's something I don't know. Surely the hospital would tell me the actual reason why I'm here, right? I'm eighteen and since I lost my memory they have to fill me in on what happened, right? Either Elizabeth's botox and fancy face creams are getting to her head, or someone is lying to me about why I'm here and what happened to me. I need to get hold of my phone once Elizabeth leaves. Maybe I could find something there?

"Don't look so confused, hun," she said. "That face you're making is bad for your skin; you don't want to get wrinkles."

"Got it," I said.

It didn't take much more meaningless small talk for Elizabeth to finally leave. I didn't expect her to stay as long as she did; she usually gets bored of my presence quite quickly.

Around noon, Crystal came in to check on me. "I haven't heard from you all day," she said.

"Sorry," I said while looking up at her. "I've just been trying to relax."

"Don't worry it's more than okay!" she said. "You definitely need your rest!"

"I guess you could say that," I giggled.

"Do you want to go down to lunch soon?"

"Yes, I would love to."

"Okay, I'll get you a walker," she said. She turned around and left the room.

Crystal returned a few minutes later with my walker. She moved my feet to the side of the bed and helped me stand up. That was the moment I realized I hadn't taken my medication the night before. I made a mental note that I needed to begin taking it tonight and continued on. Crystal held my hands as I made my way to the walker; then we made our way down the hallway, into the elevator, and down to the cafeteria. I ate light today, still assuming I should slowly ease my body back into eating normally. I got some fruit and a slice of grilled cheese. With Crystal's help, I made it to a table and ate my lunch.

After lunch, the rest of my day went by quickly. I took some of my daytime pain medication and I spent the majority of the day watching TV. I checked the news. There was an update on one of the stories from last time. It talked about the eighteen-year-old boy that was randomly attacked with a fishing hook by a lake just outside of the city. As I said, New York can be gruesome. After watching the news, I began aimlessly flipping through the guide looking for something to pass the time and keep myself occupied while I relaxed.

I ended up getting lost in my thoughts of last night. What *happened?* I asked myself. Who was that boy? Why could I walk? Was that real or am I delusional? If it wasn't real, was it a dream? If it was a dream, why did it feel so *comfortably real?*

I'd put my thoughts on pause when I noticed a presence in the doorway. I glanced to my right and saw Lucas.

"Hey, Lucas!" I said.

"Hey, how are you doing?" he asked.

"I'm doing alright, I mean I still can't walk but I'm managing. How about you?"

"I'm doing a whole lot better. This is my last night here. I got cleared to go back to school."

"Wow, that's awesome! I'm so glad for you! Are you going to be able to start playing football again?"

"Well, that's something that's to be determined. As of right now, I'll just be on the sidelines, but I found out the school has been working pretty diligently to figure out ways to keep me on the team."

"That's awesome! I'm really glad they are doing this for you!" The conversation paused. I looked out the window and indulged in the silence. When I looked back at him, he was blatantly staring at the board on the wall with all of my information. "So, you're leaving huh? It must be nice to get out of here!" I said.

"I mean yeah, I'm glad to start going back to my normal life," he said.

"I get that for sure. Hopefully, I'll be able to walk soon!"

"Yes, I hope you can walk soon. I have to get going but I happened to walk by and figured I would say bye to you before I left. So, uh, I hope you feel better soon, and good luck with your college process."

"Thank you so much! I hope everything works out with your school!"

We said our final goodbyes and he left. I was glad to hear that he was feeling better and was heading back to school, although I still had my doubts about NYU being the place for me. A few more hours passed by of me trying to find something to watch while thinking about what happened before Elizabeth was here. Maybe all that was a dream? If it was a dream though, why did it feel so real and why is it sticking with me like this?

I am currently enrolled in a psychology class at school, the latest of many I've taken over the past few years. Over time, I have been able to figure out how brains work; brains in general and mine specifically. The one thing I don't know much about is dreams. I think that's because psychologists themselves don't know much about them. Many people have their suspicions. Some people think that dreams are your wildest desires, some think they're your imagination taking over, some think they're ways for your brain to cope with trauma, some think they're a glimpse of your life in a parallel universe, and some think they're a combination of these things. Some people look into dreams deeply. I've seen charts that decipher what certain symbols mean in a dream, what certain letters mean or what certain initials mean. I have never had a dream that has felt this real or this comfortable. If last night wasn't a dream there is still no possible explanation for who this guy is, how he got here, and how I got back into my bed.

Around four I called Crystal to help get me to the shower. While washing up, I noticed a weird bruise on my leg. It was on the inside of my thigh and bright blue and purple. I tried looking to see if there was a definite impact point where the skin was hit, but it was all such a deep color that I couldn't tell. I don't remember hitting anything since I've been conscious, so that must have come from the accident. It hasn't been sore, and I don't know how I got it.

I finished washing up and got myself dressed. My walker was sitting outside of the shower room, so I switched my support system from the wall to the walker and made my way back to my room. Crystal was gone, but I assumed she had somewhere else to be.

I got back to my room and shut off the lights. The outside was dark, meaning the New York City skyline was as clear as ever. I made my way to the bed and got myself comfortable. I lay down on my side and looked at the shining lights outside. I know I've lived in New York my whole life, but for some reason, I have never had the opportunity to look at the skyline from a place where I could see it perfectly. My mind drifted to when my mother took me to see the Statue of Liberty right after my parents' divorce. I was so impressed by how tall the statue stood. My mom did a great job of harvesting my amazement and curiosity. She started spewing off facts that I still remember to this day. She told me about how the statue was a gift from the French in the late nineteenth century: how it came shipped in just over two hundred crates, how the French paid for the statue itself, and how Americans paid for the base.

In my eyes, everything the statue stands for reminds me of my mom. My mom gave me the freedom to be a curious child and encouraged my dire need to know more about the world. She gave me the freedom to learn who I was, to learn what I believe on my own, learn what I like and what I don't like. She didn't tower over me; instead, she gave me the freedom to grow up the way that I felt comfortable. This didn't make her a bad mom or a neglectful parent.

She was always there, whenever I got a cut or a scrape, or to stop me when I tried doing something that was potentially dangerous. When my underdeveloped brain couldn't solve a problem, she was always there to help me. When I needed someone to play dress-up with, someone to find me when I wanted to hide in hide-and-go-seek, or when I needed an audience for the singing shows I would perform in the living room, she was always there. She was always ready to come find my hiding spot in the house, always ready to put on her favorite dress, and always ready to be in the front row of my audience. When I wanted someone to watch my cartoons with me, she would sit on the couch next to me. When I needed someone to hug in the middle of the night because there was a thunderstorm outside and I was scared, she was always at my bedroom door. My mom was just built to be a mom.

Sometimes I wish I had a different father. Don't get me wrong, I love my father, but his workaholic tendencies forced my mother to parent me and my siblings all by herself. My mom thrived when she took the role of a single mother, but imagine if she had a partner that would parent with her. What if my dad also played hide-and-go-seek with us, or put on his best suit when we would play dress-up? What if he sat with my mom during my singing shows or what if he performed with me? What if he acted like more of a husband and a dad and less of a roommate?

Getting older with my dad around was weird. He expected a lot from me but never helped me get to where he wanted me if I was falling short. Math was never my strong suit, which he knew. He would get me a tutor from time to time if I was struggling really badly, but other than that he would make dinner awkward by judging me for my inability to understand how letters fit into math and why I need to know geometry.

When I began dating Alec, I thought for sure he was going to be mad. After all, I was pretty young and I'm my dad's youngest. He didn't have much to say, though. He just told me to be smart, don't get pregnant, and don't get hurt. Part of me almost wished he had scolded me a little bit. Part of me wished he had told me that he wanted to meet Alec before he could allow me to date him, or that boys are no good and I should rethink my decision. My father's lack of emotion towards his little girl growing up and getting a boyfriend made me feel the way my mom must have. I was turning into his roommate, rather than his daughter.

My thoughts were interrupted once more by Crystal, coming to ask if I wanted to go down to dinner. I pulled myself out of bed and held onto my walker. We made our way down the hall, to the elevator, and to the cafeteria.

For dinner tonight I had pasta with meatballs and red sauce. I sat with Crystal while eating, although her brain seemed to be scattered. The cafeteria was completely filled with staff, security, and patients. Crystal and I began a discussion, but she was in and out, focusing on me and everyone else in the room.

"So, how are you feeling, Adelynn?" she asked.

"I'm feeling alright," I responded. "The pain meds have helped a bunch I think."

"Good, I'm glad to hear that. How do you like Joyce?"

"I've only met with her once, but so far I like her."

"I'm glad to hear that. I figured she would be a good match for you."

"How much longer do you think it will take for me to be able to walk on my own?"

"I would assume probably a few more weeks. Once winter break is over for school you should be good to go back. Speaking of school, your teachers will be bringing your work soon, so you can begin working on that when you're starting to feel better too."

"That sounds good, thank you."

Her attention quickly fell onto another patient, so I finished my pasta and used my walker to slowly make my way back to my room. When I got back, I was exhausted from making my way there alone, so I lay in bed, pulled up the blankets, and got comfortable. I got some water with the help of a nurse in the hall and took my medications. I rolled over, played with my necklace, and looked at the skyline as I began falling asleep.

———

CHAPTER SEVEN

Brickyard Pond

THERE HE WAS again, walking towards my bed. He stood at the edge of my bed and smiled at me. He had a black v-neck t-shirt that made his gold chains very visible. His smile was warm and welcoming; his green eyes stared into mine. He took my hand and I got out of bed. Without saying anything, we ran out the door of my hospital room and down the hall. We were running through a completely empty hospital. Crystal and Marissa were nowhere to be found. No one was there to stop us and no one was there to witness our escape. Leaving this place with him felt...right. His hand fit into mine so comfortably and his confidence in knowing exactly where he was taking me, even if I didn't, was thrilling.

We got to the elevator and stepped in. He clicked on the button for the ground floor and we started moving. I noticed the freedom of movement I had once again. I looked down and I was standing upright without a walker and with no discomfort. My legs weren't shaky and my body felt strong. The elevator dinged and he grabbed my hands as the door opened. Before we stepped out of the elevator, he looked at me and pulled a set of car keys out of his pocket. I smiled and we ran out of the elevator, through the empty hospital lobby, and straight out the main door. As we were running, he guided me up a set of stairs across the empty street in front of the hospital entrance. We made our way up the stairs and in the first spot on the second floor of the parking garage sat a black mustang. The shiny black car had a red stripe flowing up the hood, over the roof, and all the way over the trunk. He looked at me, pulled out the keys once again, and unlocked the doors. He guided me around to the passenger side and opened the door, letting me in.

The interior of the car was a deep red. He had an evil eye pendant hanging from the rearview, strung on a piece of black twine. He got into the car and started the engine. We drove out of the parking lot and off we went. Where we were going was a mystery. I had no clue where we were driving or what we were going to be doing, but he was driving fast and looking good as he was doing so. I felt comfortable with him. I trusted that he wasn't going to hurt me and just his presence alone was enough to calm any rational thought of fear. I looked out my window and watched the street signs whiz by as we sped down Park Ave in New York City. 103rd Street, 104th Street, 105th Street, 106th Street, 107th Street, 108th Street, I thought to myself while reading the street signs as we drove through the empty street. When I glanced back at him, I noticed a tattoo on his right arm, beginning just under his wrist and ending just below the elbow. The tattoo was a depiction of the radius and ulna arm bones with a snake intertwined between the two. I didn't notice his tattoo last night; perhaps it was new. The silence in the car was comfortable, so instead of asking him about it, I looked out the window once more as the engine roared and we continued speeding down Park Ave.

It took what I interpreted as roughly forty minutes for the car to stop at our destination. The sky was a bright blue with no clouds and a bright sun that was blocked by the trees. I looked around for some sort of sign indicating where we were, but found nothing. The ground he parked on was all dirt with a small rocky dirt walkway that led through the trees. He got out of the car, came to open my door, and offered his hand as I got out. I stood for a second, admiring the landscape around me. He shut the door behind me and walked me to the path without taking his eyes off me. We were partway down the rocky dirt path, going slightly downhill, when it started to seem familiar. We ended up at a pondside area with a small concrete walkway and wall when I realized that I'd been here before. The pond's name is Brickyard Pond, and I came here nearly a million times with my mom when I was extremely young, maybe two or three. I stood there admiring the beauty of the pond and the simplicity of the environment. He guided me over to the concrete wall and sat down, urging me to join him. I'd sat down next to him when he began speaking.

"Welcome back," he said.

"This is insane!" I said. "I literally forgot this place existed!" I reached up to fiddle with my necklace.

"I figured," he chuckled. "Your mother took you here when you were super young, probably too young to remember."

I sat there for a few minutes in awe. My brain was absolutely dumbfounded that I almost hadn't recognized such a familiar, beautiful place I'd been to so many times. I looked across the water and saw the huge trees. I felt the gentle, crisp December air touching the skin on my cheeks, and I felt his arm around my back.

"I forgot about this place. I'm in awe," I said.

"I figured you would love it here. I come here to think a lot," he responded.

"I don't blame you," I smiled. "It's a beautiful place to come and think."

"Not many people know about this place, and I think that adds to the beauty of it. I mean sure, the loud city with the bright lights is gorgeous, but this is *ethereal*. Sometimes the business of the city can dampen your view of the world, do you agree?"

I paused for a second, thinking. "Yes," I responded, "I think you are right."

"What do you think are the best or worst parts of human nature?" he asked.

Well, that got deep quickly, but I had an answer for him. "I think the worst part of human nature is the way we are often filled with and taught to hate."

"What about the best part?"

"Uhmm." What exactly *is* the best part of human nature? Is there even a good part of human nature? "I don't have an answer for you there."

"Really? I get that," he said. "I think it's interesting that we are all preconditioned to hate each other but when we are born we are encouraged to think that the world is all sunshine and happiness, but *then* as we get older we are encouraged to establish the understanding that the world isn't perfect and are taught that humans are awful creatures."

"I guess I never really thought about it before, but you're right. I'm honestly drawing a blank on good traits of human nature. Maybe that's because I've always been taught that there are none."

"I'm surprised you're drawing a blank. You are a thinker, I admire that but I can't believe I stumped you. What about nature vs. nurture? Do you think that individuals are formed because of the environment or their genes?"

"I would say it's a mixture of both. I think that some things are genetic and some are based on the person's environment. I don't know what parts of development fall into what, but I think that it's a mixture of both. My mom lost her father before she was born, but my grandmother always said that she had similar mannerisms as he did. She would throw her hands in the air the same way he did when he was upset. My mom never met anyone that did that, but her father did and so did she, even though she never met him. My grandmother even said that it was easy for her to tell what my mom wanted when she was a baby because she would act like her late husband. Because she could understand his mannerisms, she could understand my nonverbal mom."

"I think you are right. I think humans are products of everything they encounter. We are presented with a particular set of traits and then what we learn and go through works with that genetic basis to create who we are in the end."

I smiled and looked out across the water.

"Do you feel uncomfortable?" he asked me.

"No, of course not," I responded. I felt comfortable with him and it felt like he knew that. The question was unnecessary; he already knew my answer. I think he just wanted to hear me say it. "If I was uncomfortable I wouldn't have left the hospital with you."

"You're strong and brave," he said. "That's very admirable."

"And you're not?" I asked.

"I am whatever you want me to be. If you think I am strong, I am strong. If you think I am weak, I am weak. If you think I am confident, I am confident. I will conform to what you want me to be. I have to for you."

My brain couldn't process that response. *What the* hell *does that mean*? I was prodded back into reality when he looked over at me and my eyes met his.

"So, what am I, Adelynn Grace Davis? What do you want me to be?"

I guess it was the perfect question. I guess that's what he wanted me to hear. He wants to charm me and make me think that he is perfect. He wants to be whatever my idea of perfection is. Why he would do this, I'm not sure. Why would someone blatantly disregard themselves and mold themselves to be your idea of perfection? He could sense I was puzzling over his words again, so I came up with a simplistic answer. "You are confident and you are *truthful*."

"Truthful was not something I was expecting, but alright Adelynn. I am confident just like you, and I am truthful."

Before I could get a thought going, he changed the conversation.

"The water is calm. Probably warm. We will go in the next time we come here. I think you would like that. Am I wrong?"

The thought of taking a swim with him ran through my mind and relaxed me in a way. To me, that sounded perfect. I looked back at him and saw him smiling. He reached his hand down to touch the water. His fingertips glided across the surface, starting a subtle spread of ripples. Every movement he made was shown in his reflection. I noticed something under his shirt. Another tattoo perhaps? That idea led me to ask him about the one I'd noticed when we were in the car.

"I like your tattoo," I paused. "The one on your arm."

"Thank you. Do you have any?"

"No."

"I have a few."

"Oh. Why did you get that one? The snake on your arm?"

"Snakes represent a few different things. Evil power and chaos, or life and healing. It's a perspective tattoo."

"So it represents what the viewer wants it to represent?"

"Exactly," he said.

The birds in the trees began to sing. I looked up and saw the cloudless sky peeking between the tips of the trees. I felt a little nudge on my right shoulder; it was him urging me to look where he was pointing. I followed his finger and saw a white bird swimming on the water in the middle of the lake.

"It's a snowy egret," he said.

"It's gorgeous."

"Let's name it."

"It has to have a pretty name."

"We will give it a pretty name."

We sat there for a while thinking on what exactly we wanted to name our bird. I eventually came up with the name Maisie, and it stuck. I felt kinda silly. Here we were, two teenagers sitting by a lake naming a bird we happened to see. The chances of me seeing Maisie again were slim, but in that moment, the time we sat there thinking about names for this bird, it felt right.

"Hopefully Maisie will be here when we come back," he said. "I like our bird."

"Me too," I giggled.

"Speaking of, I need to go." He placed his hand on my lower back and looked me in the eyes. "I will love you tomorrow, Adelynn."

_____

CHAPTER EIGHT

Potential Clues

OPENED MY EYES and saw Crystal looking at me. "Good morning, sunshine."

"Good morning, Crystal."

She walked over to the windows and opened the curtains. "I'm sorry to come in and wake you, but we have a brain scan scheduled for you today. We need to see how your head is doing."

"Is there something potentially wrong?" I asked.

"Not necessarily, but because of the severity of the accident, we want to monitor your brain activity."

Severity? The accident was *severe?* "Severity?" I asked.

She walked over to the bed and pulled my legs over so they dangled off the side. She got my walker and placed it in front of me. "Oh right, you still don't know what happened. Don't worry love, after the scan I can talk to you about what happened, but for the time being, we have to get you to the scan."

I stood up, held onto the walker, and off we went. She walked with me out of the room and helped me towards the elevator. We didn't have to wait long; she clicked the "up" button and the doors opened. She first brought me to the cafeteria so I could have breakfast, and then we headed downstairs for my scan.

This time when we stepped in the elevator she hit the button for the third floor. The entire time it was moving, she and I stood there in utter silence. The elevator dinged, the doors opened, and she helped me out into a bright white hallway. As we walked down the hallway, we passed rooms with huge table scanning machines. A few of the rooms had curtains covering the windows to the hallway and their lights off, which I guessed meant they were in the process of scanning someone. We got to Room 306A and Crystal opened the door. The room was very simplistic, with bright white walls, a huge MRI machine in the middle, and a computer set up in the corner.

"Alright Adelynn, we're gonna do an MRI scan. Sit down and another nurse will come in soon to get you started. I will come get you when you are done!"

"Thank you," I said. "Do you think you could grab my phone while I have my MRI?"

"Yes! I'll go grab that for you!"

Crystal opened the door and left. I sat down and began fidgeting with my necklace. I had never had to get an MRI before, so this would definitely be an experience for me. Time ticked by, until half an hour later the door opened and a man stepped in. He had a dark complexion, dark hair, light eyes, and was very, very tall. He had a white lab coat on with khakis. He walked over to the chair at the computer desk and sat down.

"Hello, you are Adelynn, correct?

"Yes."

"Alright, perfect. Adelynn, my name is Michael and I am going to be working with you for this MRI scan. It will be super-duper simple and I will show you what your brain looks like at the end. I think you may find that cool."

"Okay," I responded.

"Alright, well if you are ready to begin, I am as well. If you could just lie back and place your head on the pillow for me, I'm going to remove your walker from the room because we can't have any other metal objects in here while the scan is running."

He took my walker and placed it outside. He then stepped back in the room and picked up two sheets that were sitting on the shelf under the computer desk. He came over to me and spread the two white sheets over the majority of my body, leaving just my head and neck exposed.

"Alright Adelynn, can you take your necklace off?" I nodded yes and I reached up to unfasten it. I handed it to him and he put it in the drawer of his computer desk. "Alright, so these sheets I put on are to protect your body and make sure we can get an accurate scan of your head. All I need you to do is remain still and keep your eyes closed. The table you are lying on is going to move into the machine and then it is going to stay still while the machine scans you. You won't be touched by the machine or anything weird like that, so when you are ready to begin we can start." He stepped towards the computer and began typing.

"I'm ready," I said.

"Alright." He typed for a few more seconds. "Close your eyes now."

Within a few seconds, I felt the table begin to move toward the machine. I closed my eyes when the movement stopped. I lay there for about fifteen minutes and could sense the red laser moving up my face, over my eyes, and back down. Once the scan was over, the table moved outwards and I opened my eyes again. He clicked a few buttons on the computer and the machine shut off.

"Alright, so that's all done! Would you like to see it?"

"Sure." I sat up on the table and he turned the screen around so I could see the images from where I was sitting. On the screen was a picture of my brain.

"So the results will be interpreted within the next twenty-four hours but from what I can see, everything so far looks normal. You should have your results within the next week. " He pointed to the front part of my head in the image. "So this is where your frontal lobe is." He moved his hand back towards the center of the picture. "This is your parietal lobe, and layered underneath that is your temporal lobe." His finger moved to the back of my head on the image. "And finally here is your occipital lobe, pretty cool huh?"

"Yeah, that is pretty awesome!"

"Alright," he said, "so I'm gonna take the disc that these photos are on and I'm going to have Crystal come get you. Do you have any questions for me?"

"No, I think I'm all set, thank you!" He took my necklace out of the desk and gave it back to me. He then clicked some buttons, removed a disc from under the computer desk, and left. Time seemed to move so slowly. I sat in the room for an hour waiting for Crystal to return, but she was a no-show. I could have tried to make it back to my room all by myself, but my walker was still out in the hall, and I wasn't risking a fall to go get it. I waited forever for the door to open, and when it finally did, the door was opened by a female nurse that wasn't Crystal.

The nurse was maybe the age of twenty-five with short blonde hair and a light complexion. She was followed by a boy dressed in a hospital gown. He had short black hair, a light complexion, and a face that was all torn up. He had a few stitches in the skin right above his left eye and a pretty bruised lip.

"Oh, hello!" the woman said.

"Uh, hi," I said.

"Hold on one second Brady," she said as she motioned for the boy to step back out into the hallway. He stepped out and she shut the door behind her. "What is your name?" she asked me.

"I'm Adelynn."

"Did you have an MRI, Adelynn?"

"Yes, I was scanned about an hour ago."

"Alright, and do you know who brought you here and who worked with you?"

"My nurse Crystal brought me here and Michael completed the scan."

"Alright sweetheart, give me one moment." The nurse slipped out of the room and closed the door behind her. Did Crystal forget about me?

A few minutes went by and the door opened once more. This time, Michael walked in. He pulled my walker in from the hallway and brought it over to me. "I'm so sorry Adelynn. I told Crystal you were done and to assist you back to your room, but I guess she forgot. I will help you get back upstairs."

"That's alright," I responded. "Thank you."

He helped me stand up with the walker and held the door for me as I made my way out of the room. The blonde nurse and beat-up boy were standing in the hallway, waiting outside the MRI room. I made my way past them and Michael and I walked down the hallway as the nurse and boy went into the MRI room.

"Alright let's get you back to your room."

"Thank you, again."

"Of course!" Slightly awkward silence overcame us as we made it down the hallway. We got to the elevator and he clicked the up button. As we waited for the elevator he started talking to me again.

"So, you seemed like you knew what I was talking about when I showed you that scan."

"Yes," I responded. "I've taken tons of psychology classes in school, so I know a decent amount about that stuff."

"That's awesome!" he said.

The elevator dinged and we both stepped in. We made it back to my room, and he asked for permission to come in. I said yes. He helped me get onto the bed and put the walker next to it in an easily accessible spot. He seemed like a way better caretaker than Crystal, but that's just my two cents.

"Alright, can I shut the door, Adelynn? I know this may be a little uncomfortable but my coworkers needed me to ask you a few questions."

"Yeah, go for it."

He shut the door and turned towards me, keeping his distance from my bed.

"Alright, so basically I just needed to have a private conversation with you about Crystal since she essentially left you. Has she been a good nurse?"

"Uhm," I felt bad. I don't wanna throw this girl under the bus. She's been a fine nurse, but obviously her head is a little scattered. She literally left me in a strange room for an hour, knowing I needed to get back to my own and was unable to do so myself, so I figured it was better if I was honest with him. "She's fine. I mean my needs are met so I guess that makes her a good nurse. I'm not happy that I got left in a room or that sometimes her brain gets a little scattered, but she's busy so I get it I guess."

"Alright. Thank you. Just be careful Adelynn, okay? I can't say anything to you about Crystal, but just be careful. Use your intuition."

"Thank you, Michael."

He opened the door and stepped out of the room. I have absolutely no clue where that came from but I am not surprised. I think it's convenient that Crystal left after saying she would tell me the truth about what happened. Maybe it was because I asked her for my phone? Regardless, I don't have the energy to process any of that right now. I lay in bed, staring blankly at the ceiling for a few minutes, and then clicked the button on my bed, deciding to sit up a little more and turn on the TV.

A few hours went by and I watched TV undisturbed until I got a knock on the door. I'd grabbed the remote to turn down the volume when Crystal came in, followed by Elizabeth. Why on earth Elizabeth was here was beyond me, but she walked in and sat down in the chair across from my bed. Crystal left the room without saying anything to me or glancing at me once.

"Hello my dear sweet stepdaughter," she said.

"Hello...Elizabeth."

"How are you doing? How is the bruise on your leg that you got from the *car accident?*"

Why was she saying that like that? How did she know about the bruise? I decided to play along in hopes I could figure out what she wanted from me. "I'm feeling alright! What bruise on my leg? There's a bruise on my leg?"

"Yes, Crystal was telling me that the *accident* resulted in a bruise. You didn't notice it?"

"Nope, apparently not. I'll look and see if it's still there when I shower later."

"Alright. Have you gotten any work from your teachers?"

"Not yet. I'm still waiting."

"I'm sure they will give you something to do soon."

"I don't doubt it."

The room went quiet, and once again it didn't take her long to leave. Why she drove all this way to ask me two questions is beyond me, unless she had alternate intentions. Still, my brain did not want to process any of this, so I turned the volume back up on my TV and continued watching my show.

Around noon, the news came on. The first story was absolutely heart-wrenching. A husband and wife were accused of operating a sex trafficking ring. The next story was about a murder. A father was shot when his daughter called for help because she got into a fight with her ex-boyfriend on 105th Street late last night.

I shut the news off quickly. Sometimes New York is so overwhelmingly violent, and with my physical and mental state right now, processing the outside world is too much for me. Unsure of where Crystal and I stood, I swung my legs off the side of the bed, grabbed my walker, and made my way to the board with my information. I used my index finger to erase the words "high fall risk" and "low mobility" from my chart. I then turned around with my walker, made my way to the door, and headed down to the cafeteria.

The cafeteria was a lot quieter than usual. I made my way over to the counter and picked up a plate with a ham and cheese sandwich on it. I got a cup of apple juice and sat at the nearest table. I looked up and saw the boy that was getting an MRI sitting across from me. He noticed I was looking at him and he attempted a smile, although his lip was so swollen he wasn't entirely successful. He got up and came over to me.

"Hey! Sorry, is it okay if I sit here?"

"Yes, of course!"

"I'm Adelynn," I said.

"I'm Brady," he answered.

"How are you doing? Are you alright?"

"Yeah, just a little bruised up, obviously," he chuckled.

"Right, haha."

"Did you ever make it back to your room?" he asked.

"Yeah, that whole thing was a really bizarre situation. I guess my primary nurse kinda just got up and left me there even though she knew I couldn't walk without my walker."

"I'm really sorry to hear that. That's no fun."

"It really wasn't but it's no big deal. You look like you're in pain; I'm not in physical pain so I guess I can't complain. If you don't mind me asking, what happened?"

"Well, it's a long story. I got into a fight trying to defend my friend. My friend Ariana and I were out when her ex came up to us and asked to talk to her. They kinda have a weird on-and-off thing going and when she was talking to him he grabbed her. I told him to get his hands off her as she pulled away and then he started yelling and attacking her. Don't let my scars fool you though—I intervened and I won."

"Oh wow, that's insane. Why are you here then? Are they trying to treat your wounds or something?"

"Well, when fighting I hit my head, so they just wanted to make sure my head's alright. Hopefully, I'll be out of here in no time."

"I hope everything is alright, are any charges going to be filed?"

"He was arrested because he put his hands on her before I intervened. I don't know what he will be charged with but I hope he gets charged for something and it puts him away for good. He's really abusive to her and super toxic."

"That's awful." Suddenly, I felt everything coming back. Feelings of fear and absolute helplessness coursed through my veins. The thought of how Alec touched me, how he would always have his way. How my opinions and my being were unworthy in his eyes. The fear as he came near me during a fight. The helplessness that overtook me when he got me in a room alone. I began fidgeting with my necklace and I could feel my hand shaking. Brady looked at me like he could tell I was reliving a nightmare.

"Are you okay?"

"Yeah, I'm alright." I felt my brain begin to shut down. "J-just thinking."

He paused. I could tell he didn't know where the conversation went wrong and why I was acting the way I was. The abuse I suffered from Alec is something I've spent the last few years of my life burying. It's a topic I don't talk about. A part of me that I don't call my own. A past trauma that I disassociate from. I needed to shut off the remembrance that was flowing through my veins and change the subject, so that was exactly what I did.

"How's the chicken?" I asked him.

He looked down and smirked. "It's really good."

"Really? I have yet to try it here. I've heard good and bad things about hospital food in the past so I stick to foods that I'm comfortable with."

"Well, I would definitely recommend the lemon chicken here."

"Noted. Anything else here you would recommend?"

"Yes actually. I haven't been here long but I had the crepes this morning with strawberries and blueberries and it was so good. I would definitely recommend it."

"That's good to know, thank you!"

He finished his plate at about the same time I decided I was done eating.

"Are you finished?"

"Yeah."

"Do you want me to help you with your walker; you didn't come down with your nurse did you?"

"I honestly don't know where my nurse is or where I stand with her, but I think I've got it. Thank you."

"Yeah, of course. I'll see you around!"

"See ya!"

I maneuvered over to the garbage to throw away my leftover food while he sat and finished his drink. I made my way out of the cafeteria and about twenty minutes later, I was back in my room. I went over to the bed and sat down.

Soon, I began thinking about *him*, the boy from my dream. I don't even know his name. How did he know about Brickyard Pond? How did he know that I was brought there when I was younger? It made me feel a billion different emotions, thinking about him. Where did this boy come from? He *has* to be a dream, right? There's no way he can exist? What if he does exist? Does he go to school with me and I just never noticed him? Maybe he's in college instead? Maybe he lives in a different town and we have mutual friends? All of these questions and no answers. All of these scenarios and not even one makes sense.

How strange it was that I felt comfortable with him. I wasn't the least bit alarmed with him taking my hand and leading me out of this place. When you are young, parents always tell you to be careful of strangers, but what if a stranger isn't really a stranger? What if a stranger doesn't *feel* like a stranger. His essence feels familiar, and that makes me think that maybe he isn't a stranger. It leads me back to the question of whether or not he is real. *I have to get his name.* I need to know the name of the stranger that doesn't feel like a stranger. Perhaps, if I know his name, I can justify my fascination with him because then he won't be a stranger.

How silly it was to me. It felt so silly knowing that I could sit there and watch the sky with someone. Silly that I could sit there and learn about zodiac signs when I never cared much about them. Silly that I felt comfortable dancing on a hospital rooftop with a boy I had never met before and with no background music. Silly that I felt comfortable naming birds with someone. That is something that many people would see as childish, but I felt comfortable, like it was appropriate. It was such a mind-blowing concept. The concept that comfort was something I never interpreted it to be. I've never been comfortable with a presumed stranger and I've never felt comfortable allowing my inner child to be free in someone else's presence.

———

CHAPTER NINE

Trapped in Thought

THROUGHOUT GRADE SCHOOL, I was told that the brain is an organ that can change the world. I've also been told by many that I don't think the same way as others. I was fortunate enough to have teachers that took the time to understand how I think and to help me figure out the way my brain works.

I think about things that most people don't often think about. I know it may sound dumb, but the majority of my free time is spent thinking about questions that most people would never ask themselves.

Is free will real, or is it just an illusion? Recently, I have altered my answer to this question, changing my stance completely on the topic. There are things that we control. Surely there have to be. Does the universe control our lives? I think yes. I think free will and the will of the universe coexist. Bigger events, like the way your love life works out over the rest of your life, have to have some sort of universal influence. However, if I do something insignificant, I believe it may be a different case. If I get lazy one day and decide not to wash my hair and my hair gets greasy for example, that has to just be a product of a small decision I made that has nothing to do with the universe. But, losing your ability to do something and then finding a new and better passion, going through a rough breakup and then ending up finding someone better, or even not getting a job that you wanted and then ending up finding a better job has to be the work of the universe. Big changes are the idea that everything happens for a reason at work, but the small decisions like what cereal to eat for breakfast, when to wash your hair, and whether or not to get coffee, all have to be the work of something that isn't the universe. That has to be the will of one's own self.

It's deep, I know, but my mind goes deeper. *What is the meaning of life? Why do we exist?* The universe is vast. The universe is constantly expanding. But here we are. Existing. Living. Moving. Working. Why? The little insignificant things in our day that we control don't add up to anything significant in the vast universe. Perhaps the things that the universe has planned for us play a larger role than our free thought, but even then the universe is so vast that it couldn't even amount to that much. Whether or not you talk to your crush, or if you are bold and tell the people around you that you love them, or do anything that is seen as risky in our society does not matter. With that being said, perhaps we weren't supposed to find out about the universe and space. Maybe the small and big problems and situations we encounter were supposed to be the only thing our human race knows. Maybe we know too much?

Where is nothing and what is it? Alright, so I'm right outside of New York City. I'm in the United States of America, in North America. North America is a continent on Earth and the Earth is part of the solar system. The solar system is part of the galaxy, the galaxy is part of the universe. Now, where is the universe? Well, there's nothing else after you reach the end of the universe, correct? Well, then what is nothing and where is it? What is the universe in and where is that place of nothing that it is located at the end of it?

Does fate exist? A loaded question in the form of three words. It stems from the question of whether the universe has an impact on our lives. Fate only exists if the universe impacts some or all of our decisions. If the universe does not have an impact on what we do here on Earth, then it can't have an impact on our future, and fate doesn't really exist. This question is the trickiest for me to think about because the more I think about it, the more it twists my brain and the more I confuse myself. If you ask Peyton, she would say that the universe does affect us because she claims herself to be a medium, but I just can't seem to find my stance on this particular question.

Does the Law of Attraction exist? For reference, I would define the law of attraction as the ability to attract outcomes that match our attitudes, positive or negative. Is there a way for us to manifest what we want? If the universe has some sort of control, then no. If the universe doesn't have some sort of control, then also no. If the universe has a say over what we do, then no matter how hard we positively hope for something, it won't happen. If the universe doesn't have a say over what we do, then thoughts are just that, thoughts. Nothing else knows what we are thinking and there is nothing in our universe to make events manifest in connection with our thoughts.

Does "don't jinx it" really make sense? We've all experienced it, whether it was in elementary school on the playground, at a sleepover, or anywhere else really. If you say something that is not expected to happen but might yet happen, chances are someone will respond with "well, don't jinx it." This term seriously implies that the universe will alter the future or a series of events all because someone mentions that something has yet to happen. If you try to follow the logic behind that, it really doesn't make sense, now does it?

Is the butterfly effect real? This question really boggles my brain, because butterflies are so simple, but the butterfly effect is a very complex thing to think about. It's very weird to think about: the idea that something will happen to someone you don't know, perhaps someone on the other side of the world, because of the small indirect decisions one makes in their day-to-day life.

Does everything really happen for a reason? I've searched long and hard to try and figure out an answer to this question, and to my initial surprise, I have to say yes. Yes it does. Everything happens for a reason. I realized this in the smallest areas in my life.

Will the world ever really end? If it does, what does the "end of the world" do to our solar system? I have already been flipping back and forth with the idea that the universe probably doesn't really care about us here on Earth. If the world as we know it ends and all humans go extinct, the universe will still continue on. The planets will still spin and rotate and Earth will be just fine. It'll just be rid of humans and maybe even life. The most mind-boggling thing about this is none of us will be around to see it happen; if it does happen, none of us can escape it or stop it.

Can anyone really know their true self? I typically find myself constantly asking myself questions about myself. If you really can know your true self, I would say I'm the closest out of the human population to doing so. As I have mentioned, I have spent a long time trying to explain things that many people don't usually think about, which also means that during that process I have done a lot of self-reflection and figured out my stance on every logical and illogical question. I like to think that I know myself inside and out, but whether that's really possible is the main question. I think it is? When someone says they know their best friend or their partner inside and out I always get the urge to roll my eyes. You could be with someone for years and still learn things about them. Hell, individuals can be in their late eighties and still be learning things about themselves... which brings me to some self-reflection questions next.

Are you an introvert or an extrovert? Both. As suggested by the previous question, this answer is very easy for me. I am extroverted when I am feeling energized and comfortable. If I feel comfortable in the crowd I am in, I could spend hours talking to someone. If I am feeling drained and uncomfortable, it doesn't usually end with me sitting next to someone and talking about myself for three hours. It really just boils down to how I feel at the moment.

Do you believe in second chances? I obviously believe that second chances are possible, but I will personally never give someone a second chance. I just feel like if someone genuinely has good intentions, they will never find themselves in a second-chance position.

What is your biggest mistake in life and what did you learn from it? Alec. Letting someone take control of my body. Giving him my power. Lesson learned: TBD.

What did your past relationship teach you? Again, lesson learned: TBD.

Why is love so personal? It's unnecessary for love to be as personal as it is. People love and then hate the person later on because their love didn't work out. If soul mates exist, why do people get so hurt when love ends? Even if someone really hurts you and they did something wrong, they aren't the one, so why can't people just be happy that the person's true colors showed and that they are one step closer to finding their person?

CHAPTER TEN

Moonlit Waves

HERE HE WAS again. He was standing in the doorway of my hospital room. He was staring out the window at the city. I copied him. The lights were as bright as ever, but for some reason, they looked a little different this time. After being in this hospital room so much and living here my whole life, I thought I had the details of the city memorized by now, but something looked different. I don't know if the Empire State Building was in a different place or if the Crescent Building's famous crescents were upside down, but something definitely looked off about the city tonight.

The silence of the room was broken when he started walking toward me. I looked over at him and he reached out his hand, indicating we would go on another adventure tonight. He was wearing a navy blue v-neck t-shirt. He had what seemed to be a leather jacket on. His gold chain sat atop the collar of his shirt and his tattoo was peeking out of his sleeve. He was smiling at me and my eyes met his. I took his hand and got out of bed, able to walk freely once again. We went down the long hallway and got into the elevator, going down to the ground floor. We left the front doors of the hospital and went up the stairs across the street. He reached into his pocket, grabbed his keys, and unlocked his car. We walked around to the passenger side, he opened my door and I got in.

Soon we were driving through the empty streets of the city. His sunroof was open, allowing me to look up and see the stars. The air was a little foggy, the sky was the darkest I've ever seen it. My hair was blowing around and dancing in the wind. He took his right hand off the wheel and held it palm up over the center console, silently asking me to grab his hand. Smooth, I thought to myself. He must think he's really something. Sitting there, looking incredible, knowing that I trust him, relaxed with one hand on the wheel taking us to God knows where. He's charming and he knows it. I gave him my hand.

We drove for what felt like forever. I would switch from looking up at the stars, to looking at him, to watching the road ahead of us, to looking out my window. We eventually made it out of the city, and we were surrounded by nothing but trees. There were no street signs anywhere. We were really in the middle of nowhere. Eventually, he turned on his left blinker and turned the car. There we were in a dirt parking lot. He parked the car, looked at me for a second, got out, and came around to get the door for me. I stepped out and immediately noticed the sound of waves crashing.

I looked around. It was dark, so there was not much I could see.

"Welcome to my place. I came here a lot when I was in college. This is another one of my thinking places," he said.

College, I thought. Did he go to college? Is he still in college? "Oh wow, this seems like a really nice place," I said, still not really knowing if it was a nice place or not because it was so dark.

"I know you can't really see much silly," he said as he pulled a flashlight out of his pocket. "Here, use this."

I turned on the flashlight and began to look around us. The next thing I knew, he grabbed my hand and started leading me towards the sound of the waves. My feet tumbled over each other, and I realized the dirt road where his car was had now turned into a path of shells and rocks surrounded by grass and brush. A few seconds later, we were walking on the sand. I paused to bend down and take off my shoes. I untied the sneakers and removed my socks as well, shoving them into my shoes and moving on. I held my shoes and the flashlight in my left hand while I gave him my right. The sand was cold. I think that's my favorite part about going to the beach at night. The sand is moldable and nice and cold. You can sink your feet into the dry, cold, comfortable sand. As we got closer to the shoreline he stopped us. I swept the flashlight back and forth to see our surroundings. There were many rocks and shells scattered throughout the sand where the water met the shore. I looked over my shoulder and stared off at the nearby lifeguard stand for a moment. He noticed and followed the direction of my stare. He then grabbed my hand and directed me to the empty stand.

When we reached the stand, I placed my shoes on the top and handed him the flashlight. He let me go up first and he held my hips as I climbed up the wooden ladder step by step. He placed the flashlight next to my shoes and climbed up after me. We both sat on the lifeguard bench. He sat on my right, putting his arm around me and making himself comfortable.

"It's a beautiful night tonight," he said.

"It really is," I responded.

"I much prefer the beach at night. There is usually no one here when it's dark. All the crowds are gone, the sand is cold and won't burn your feet, you don't have to worry about getting a sunburn, and you can hear the calming noise of the waves crashing. It's just a beautiful place to be."

His voice was calming. He really knows how to describe this place in the best way it could possibly be described. "It is pretty awesome here." The conversation fizzled out. Occasionally, he would rub my shoulder with his arm, and eventually I rested my head on his lap. He rubbed my head and played with the ends of my hair from time to time. After a long while of sitting on the lifeguard stand and minimal casual conversation, he began to move.

I sat up, and he stood up and climbed down the ladder, grabbing the flashlight on his way down. He turned back to the lifeguard stand and gestured for me to follow him. Once I'd climbed down, he placed the flashlight at the top of the ladder, turned it on, and pointed it at the area to the left of the stand. He then took off a tiny, drawstring backpack that I hadn't noticed previously, and placed it on the ground. He opened the bag and pulled out two glass mason jars. He handed me one and I unscrewed the lid. It was empty. He opened his jar and looked at me.

"So," he said, "I brought these here so we could collect rocks. I thought it would be cute since you loved collecting rocks when you were a kid, and this beach is the perfect place to do it."

How on earth did he know that? No one knows about that side of me. Prior to my parents' divorce, my favorite thing to do was collect rocks. I would collect rocks literally everywhere. Anyone that saw my rock collection must have thought I was insane because there was nothing special about any of those rocks. They were all just rocks that you could find literally anywhere. I had mainly gray rocks and I thought they were the coolest things ever. My mom had to buy clothes that had large pockets so I could store all of them, and believe me, I was not a very strong or big toddler. My little premature body had to develop the strength in my waist so I could carry all of those rocks in my pockets. But that was years ago.

I looked up at him and he turned around and signaled for me to follow. He began looking around at the ground. About a foot in front of him was a small, gray rock with a white band going through it. He picked up the rock and held it up to the flashlight beam to get a better look at it. He smiled and placed the rock in the jar.

I then began searching for my own rocks. About ten steps away from the lifeguard stand I found a beautiful and larger white rock with no imperfections. I walked back towards the flashlight and held up my find. The rock glowed under the light, so I put it at the base of my mason jar. The rock fit perfectly flush with the base. After placing it in the jar I continued my search.

Next, I came across a gorgeous shiny rock that was square shaped. It had a tan undertone with little specks of shiny minerals that made the rock shine vibrantly. My guess is the shiny minerals are mica, which I learned in environmental science freshman year is a silicate mineral. Without even walking back to the flashlight, I placed it in the mason jar where it sat on top of the white rock. I took a few steps forward and found a pebble-sized gray rock with little black and white specks covering it. I placed this pebble rock next to the mica in my jar and kept going.

The next rock was harder; I couldn't find anything that I liked. I did come across a gray medium-sized flat rock that wouldn't fit properly in my jar. I had to place it standing up and I didn't like the look of that so I removed it. I then found a small tan rock with tiny white details. The white details looked like spider webs breaking through the rock. I placed it in my jar and continued on.

Once my jar was about halfway filled, I found a beautiful tan rock that was shaped like a heart. It had little specks of miscellaneous colors, such as blue, purple, and green running throughout. In disbelief, I walked back towards the lifeguard stand to the flashlight. He did as well. I got to the flashlight and held up the rock.

"Look how cool this one is!" I exclaimed.

"Wow. That one really is spectacular," he responded.

We both smiled, and that's when I noticed his jar was completely full. He had an incredible mosaic of rocks in his jar.

"Would you like me to look with you?" he asked.

"Sure," I responded smiling.

He placed his mason jar of rocks down on the lifeguard stand and picked up the flashlight. We walked off in the opposite direction of where I was previously looking. He soon paused, looking at the ground, and picked up a medium-sized light pink rock with gray and black dots covering it. He handed the rock to me and smiled.

"I love it!" I said.

He smiled. "You should take a picture of it. It's very artsy and aesthetic," he said.

I reached for my pocket; then remembered...

"I would take a photo but I don't have my phone."

"You should get it back. Don't worry, I've got it." He pulled out a phone and I stood next to him, holding out the rock. My fingernails were painted black, but my thumb had a chip in the paint. My thumb was the only nail visible in the photo, but the photo still looked good despite the chipped nail polish. He showed the picture to me and he was right, it was very aesthetic.

I placed the rock in the jar and we continued on. The next rock was one I found. It was a beautiful whitish transparent rock that was smaller in size. My guess would be that it was quartz. I put it in my jar and continued my search. We went back and forth like this for a while. We would both find rocks and some of them I would like and put in the jar and some of them I would dislike and put back. It didn't take long until my jar was full, and we began heading back to the lifeguard stand.

Once we reached the stand, he began climbing up once more. When he lifted his arms to grab the top of the ladder, I saw yet another tattoo peeking out from under his shirt. It seemed to be on his back, and stretched from just left of his spine and wrapped around his body to about where his arm was. I couldn't make out what the tattoo was of, but I had never noticed it before.

He reached the top of the ladder and kneeled down, signaling for me to give him my jar so I could climb up. I handed him my jar and he reached for my left hand so he could help me up. Once he'd put my jar down he offered both his hands. They were pleasantly warm, which was odd because I was freezing. He could feel how cold I was and once I reached the top of the ladder, he took off his coat and put it around my shoulders. We sat down and I lay my head back on his lap again.

"Alright, so what do you think about going through our jars and telling each other why we picked the ones we did?" he said.

"That is such a cute idea. You go first," I responded.

He picked his jar of rocks up off the floor, which was when I noticed half of it was filled with sand.

"Hey! No wonder it didn't take you long to fill up your jar!" I said. "You're a cheater! Why did you also get sand?" I giggled.

He chuckled. "Well, I wanted both sand and rocks. A little bit of both from tonight's adventure with you."

I blushed. He went back to opening his jar. The first rock he pulled out was tan with a gray stripe. He explained that he picked this rock because this was the first rock he had ever seen that had tan with gray running through it, rather than the other way around. He placed the rock on the bench on his other side and pulled out another. This one was a medium-sized, completely round purplish rock. It had slight marbling with pieces of light lavender running through it. This one reminded him of the sunset, he explained. Sometimes he notices dark purples with light lavender in the sunsets. He placed this rock with the first one and continued on. Next, he pulled out a small, blue and white marbled rock. He just thought this one was cool. He put that one down and then pulled out a small, textured, algae-colored rock. He explained to me that he liked how this rock was textured and that made it different from all of the others. He then took out a smooth, medium-sized gray flat rock that fit flush on top of the sand and separated the rocks he had already shown me from the sand at the bottom. "This one was just for organization." He grinned.

"I still can't believe you got a bunch of sand," I said.

He shrugged. "As I said I wanted to have a little bit of everything from tonight's rock search. Now come on, let's see your rocks!"

"Well, you already know what half of mine look like because you helped me pick them!"

"Some of the ones I gave you didn't make it into the jar," he said.

"Okay, fine, I guess you're right."

He handed me my jar and I sat up and unscrewed the lid, pulling out the first rock. It was a perfectly round white rock that was about medium-size. "So this rock," I said, "was picked out by you for me. I decided to keep this one because I like the consistent coloration and I also like how smooth it is." I pulled the next rock from the jar. The next one was a medium-sized textured rock with an orange tint to it. "This one I picked because I didn't really have any orange and I decided to add it to spice up the aesthetic of the jar a little." The one after that was a pebble-sized, smooth, tan rock. "This one I picked because it was the perfect size to fit in the gap between that last orange rock and the next rock I'm going to show you."

"Oh, so I guess you like things to be organized huh?" he asked.

"Well, yeah. I just figured I wouldn't waste the space," I responded. The next one was a smooth, green, medium-sized rock that was slightly misshapen. "This rock I chose because I wanted to give the other green rock in here a friend." He chuckled. Then I pulled out the pink rock that we took a photo of. "I think this one is pretty self-explanatory." I then pulled out four little pebble rocks that were nearly identical. They were all a dark gray. Three of them were the same size, but one of them was slightly smaller. "You gave me two of these and I found two others that kinda matched." Now came a flat, medium-sized, smooth gray rock. "It has layers. That's why I picked it. It is probably a sedimentary rock." The next rock out of the jar was a green, smooth, round one. "I just liked the green, there's not much more of a reason than that." The next rock I pulled out was a bluish color and was similar in shape to the first green rock. "I like how this one matched the unique shape of the green rock."

By the time I finally reached the first five I had picked without him, I was kinda wishing that I hadn't picked so many rocks and done what he did with the sand. I couldn't really come up with many reasons as to why I chose the ones I did and because of that, I wondered if I was boring him. I mainly picked the ones I did because I just liked them. There wasn't much more of a reason than that. I continued on, just hoping I wasn't making him regret asking me to talk about the rocks. I pulled out the heart-shaped rock and smirked. "I think this one is also kinda self-explanatory," I giggled.

"That one is by far my favorite," he said. "I don't think I have ever seen a rock shaped like that before."

"These are my favorite ones to try and find. I think heart-shaped rocks are the coolest. I mean they have been tumbling around for probably years and it just so happens that nature made one that looks like this." His validation here made me feel a little better. Maybe I wasn't boring him after all. I pulled out the next rock and it was the black and white tiny one. "Doesn't this one look like salt and pepper?" I asked.

"Yeah, it actually really does," he smiled. "I don't think I would have ever noticed that one."

I smiled. Next, I wanted to show him the mica, so I pulled it out with excitement. "Okay, so this one, I have my suspicions it's a mica rock. I learned a lot about rocks in high school and I think these little shiny flecks are mica." He reached for the flashlight and brought it super close to the rock. The rock sparkled and reflected the light in all different directions. "So, if this is a mica rock, that means the silicate minerals that make up the layers of the mica form in very thin sheets and can sometimes be easy to pick off and very flexible." I moved my thumbnail across the surface of the rock and little pieces of mica began breaking off. "See! It's very fragile. There are about thirty-seven different types of mica minerals if I remember correctly."

"Wow, that is honestly really cool! I had no clue that was even a thing. I knew you used to collect rocks but I didn't know you knew this much about them," he said.

"I don't know that much, kinda just a thing or two." I pulled out the next rock, a small, tan, flat oval. "I just liked the texture of this one."

"I've noticed you seem to like different textures a lot, huh?" he asked.

"It's the first thing I notice when I pick up a rock," I responded. "Okay, this is my last one." He seemed to be upset that this was my last rock and I would be stopping soon. My last rock to show him was the first rock that I picked up: a white, flat rock that lay flush along the base of the mason jar. "This one I like because of the texture too."

"That was really fun. We should do more stuff like this. I love hearing you talk!" he said.

"Thank you." I could feel myself blushing. "I don't think anyone has ever said that to me before."

We began putting the rocks back into the jars. Once I had finished adding everything back, I looked at the jar, turning it around so I could see how everything looked all together inside it.

"I feel like yours is very aesthetically pleasing," he said. "You should take a picture of it with your phone. It would be a nice wallpaper."

"I already told you, I don't have my phone," I sighed. It was at that moment that I intuitively touched my jean pocket and felt the outline of my phone in it. Or rather, *a* phone; when I took it out of my pocket I realized it wasn't mine. It was a different model of the phone that I have, a different phone and case color. The password prompt came up and I typed in my password. Somehow it worked, it unlocked the phone. The next thing I know, there's a photo of Zac on my screen. It seemed like the photo I was being shown was part of a news article. I tried scrolling down using my thumb, but instead of scrolling down on the news article, it brought me back to the phone's home screen. The wallpaper was not mine. It was a photo of the city lights. I swear it was the same exact view I have from my hospital room. Once on my home screen, I noticed he was staring at me, confused. Perhaps he was curious as to why I was taking so long. That was when I clicked on the camera, held up my jar of rocks, and snapped a photo.

I lay back down, putting my head on his legs and placing the phone on my stomach, locking it as I did so. I didn't want to be on it while I was spending this time with him. I placed my jar of rocks on the floor of the lifeguard stand and looked at him. I noticed he was staring at the spot I'd placed the phone. Perhaps he was trying to see the time?

"I have to go Adelynn," he said.

"Go, where?" I asked—as if I hadn't asked him that question when he told me that before!

"Away. Just for a bit though. Adelynn, I will love you tomorrow."

CHAPTER ELEVEN

Staggered Normalcy

THE LIGHT WAS shining through the curtains as bright as ever when I woke up. I lay in bed for what felt like forever. Staring out at the city, with no desire to even attempt to sit up. Today, I woke up feeling extremely drowsy. It felt like someone hit me with a truck.

I left the TV off for a while and enjoyed the quietness of the room. That was until Crystal decided to open the door and pay me a visit after falling off the face of the earth the last few days.

"Good morning Adelynn," she exclaimed.

"Good morning Crystal."

"I have some things for you!"

"Oh, like what?"

"Homework," she smirked. She took a tote bag off her shoulder and pulled out a two-page packet along with a pencil and notepad. She placed the packet, pencil, and notepad at the base of my bed just below my feet. "This is the first of many to come. It's a short essay from your psychology teacher."

"Thanks."

"How have you been doing by the way? I know I haven't really been around much. What can I say, I'm a busy girl," she giggled.

"I've been doing alright."

"Great. Well, I'll see you later. You should get to writing," she said while winking at me. I think that was by far the weirdest interaction I have ever had with that woman, and that says a lot considering she literally left me at my brain scan without the ability to walk on my own.

I let the packet she brought me sit at the base of my bed for a few hours. I took a little bit of time to myself, enjoying the silence, and eventually switched to watching TV.

At around eleven I decided to pick up the packet and see what the prompt was. Attached with a paperclip was a sunflower sticker. I wasn't surprised that my teacher added that little touch because she loves sunflowers; she says they're a symbol of optimism. I took off the sticker and read the prompt. *What do dreams reveal about a person?* Interesting. I don't really know how to answer that question. I guess I've never thought that dreams reveal anything about a person; rather, I've thought of it the other way around. I would say that the person reveals something about their dreams; by that I mean the individual's day-to-day life, goals, desires, and actions all result in their sequence of dreams. I really had never thought about this question in this particular way before. I picked up the pencil and notepad that Crystal gave me and began writing my essay.

Adelynn Grace Davis

Mrs. Collins

Psychology 312 - Psychology of Adulthood

Everybody dreams. Dreams are not a materialistic thing, yet they are a phenomenon that we all experience. Despite their commonality, psychologists have not been able to pinpoint how or why exactly we dream.

My pen was interrupted when I felt a presence standing at my doorway. I looked up and there she was. Nevaeh. Her long blonde hair was curled and pulled back into a ponytail. Her green eyes were staring right at me. She had a full face of makeup on and if I had to guess, every one of the makeup items she's wearing cost her more than my medical bills from this hospital will once I get discharged. She had a pink mini tennis skirt on with a cable knit sweater-vest and sneakers. She looked like she had just come from her family's private resort. There was a lollipop in her hand that she quickly removed from her mouth. She began twirling the lollipop in the air and talking to me.

"Hello, Adelynn."

"How did you even get—"

"Don't worry about it. We need to chat." She stepped further into my room, shutting the door behind her. She sat down in the chair at the foot of my bed. "Well," she said as she adjusted her posture, "I'm sure you have heard by now but Alec and I have split."

"Okay. I'm sorry. I had no clue."

"Oh really," she chuckled. "So you think you can just lie to my face?"

"No, I'm being completely hone—"

"Bullshit! Why are you trying to lie to me right now?"

"Look, I haven't been on my phone or talked to anyone from the outside world for weeks so I don't entirely get how you expect me to know that you guys split. Even if I did find out I wouldn't have care—"

"Oh save it! You better stay away from him. I know what you and he are trying to do! You are trying to get back with him and he's trying to hurt me. This is all your fault."

"What are you even talking ab—"

"Just shut up, won't you! I don't want to hear another peep from you," she said as she stuck out her pointer finger directly at me. "I told you to leave him alone, now you better listen to me and take my warning." Without saying another word, she got up and left, slamming the door behind her.

That was definitely not what I was expecting. I had no clue how to feel after that encounter. How did she even know that I was here? Why does she think I've had any interactions with Alec? Even if I did have contact with Alec, what could her petite five-foot-two body do to me?

I wonder what people are hearing at school. Surely at least someone must have noticed that I've been out for an extended period of time. I wonder if the accident was on the news. I also wonder if anyone that I go to school with was with me. Or saw it? Or caused the accident?

The more time I spend in the hospital the less I know about whatever series of events got me here in the first place. I doubt Crystal would tell me if I asked her, and I don't have contact with anyone else that could fill me in. Besides, I haven't seen much of Crystal. I have mainly been doing for myself. I've been taking myself to get food on my own, taking myself to the restroom, to the shower. I still rely on my walker and I'm sure it would be nice to have an extra hand to help me get around. I wonder if I could request a different nurse. I liked having Michael assist me during my brain scan but I don't recall him being a nurse. To my knowledge, he just works on the floor where the MRIs take place. Speaking of, I still haven't gotten my lab results back yet from my scan.

I continued working on my homework for the majority of the day. I ended up skipping lunch because I didn't feel like lugging my body all the way upstairs and then all the way back to my room. I wish hospitals had takeout.

I continued working on the beginning of the essay. By the time dinner came, I was actually hungry, so I wrapped up the first paragraph of my paper, deciding to read through what I had so far and then call it a day.

Adelynn Grace Davis

Mrs. Collins

Psychology 312 - Psychology of Adulthood

Everybody dreams. Dreams are not a materialistic thing, yet they are a phenomenon that we all experience. Despite their commonality, psychologists have not been able to pinpoint how or why exactly we dream. With that being said, many believe that dreams are able to reveal a lot about an individual. Dreams are able to both reveal and reflect an individual's goals, aspirations, and fears.

Dreams reflect an individual's goals because many times, dreams can harvest what one wants and trick the brain into believing for a short period that it is living that reality.

Once I read through that, I placed all my materials at the bottom of the bed again. I got up by using my walker. I picked up the pencil, notepad, and packet and placed them on the chair before making my way out of the room and to the elevator. The cafeteria was packed. I made my way to the back of the room to get my food. Lemon chicken with a side of mashed potatoes was what I decided on; then I made my way through the hospital cafeteria crowd to find a seat.

After wandering around for a bit, I noticed Zac sitting alone at a table on the left side of the room. A spot there was my only option so I made my way over to him. I reached the table and placed my food down in the seat across from him.

"Hello! Can I sit here?"

"Hey! Sure," he answered. I sat down and got myself settled in. He had a plate of chicken Milanese sitting in front of him.

"Chicken sure seems to be popular tonight, huh?" I asked.

"I guess it is. Lemon chicken?" he asked while looking at my plate.

"Yeah! I thought it looked pretty good so I figured I would give it a shot."

"Yeah," he said.

I found I couldn't come up with anything else to say. He was in my dream last night, but why? I had the desire to get to know him, but I couldn't figure out why. My thoughts were interrupted when he continued the conversation.

"Who are your nurses while you are here?"

"I have Crystal and Marissa. Crystal is my day nurse and Marissa is my night nurse."

"No way, they are my nurses too," he said. "Have you seen much of Crystal lately?"

"I actually haven't."

"What do you think of her?"

"She's okay." I thought back to her leaving me at my brain scan and about how off she seemed the last few days. "She's been acting a little weird lately. I can't really tell why."

"That's what I was thinking too! She hasn't been coming around as much as she should be. She comes in at random times during the day and hasn't been doing a good job when she is around. I've easily got another month in this hospital. I kinda need someone to help me."

"Oh wow, she hasn't been helping me much either but I'll be out of here soon probably, and I'm healthy enough to fend for myself. Have you considered requesting a new nurse?"

"I tried. I was told no. Have you seen Crystal walking around the hallways lately, but she never comes into your room? For the last week or so she's just been pacing up and down the halls and neglecting me."

"What floor of the hospital are you on if you don't mind me asking? I could help you get around if you need help and Crystal isn't helping. I haven't seen her pacing, that's honestly so weird."

"Are you sure? I'm on floor eight."

"Yes of course! I'm on the same floor as you. It shouldn't be much of a hassle. We Crystal patients need to stick together apparently."

"Okay," he chuckled. "Can I just give you my phone number and I can use that to get in touch with you when I need help?"

"Yeah of course! I have yet to get my phone back but I can ask for it when I see Crystal next."

"Okay, that would be awesome, thank you! I'll shoot you a text and when you get your phone back just respond so I'll know you have it and I can reach you." He pulled his phone out of his pocket, unlocked it, and opened a new contact card. He put the phone on the table and slid it over to me. I placed down my fork and began typing. Adelynn (Room 829), (631) 881-9087. I slid it back across the table towards him. "Thank you."

"Has Crystal ever forgotten you somewhere? I kid you not she literally left me in the room where I got my brain scan without my walker and never came to bring me back to my room."

"Yeah actually, she has. I had to get unexpected mild surgery about a week after I got here. I was assigned to a different nurse while I was in surgery and recovering, but the day I was supposed to go to my room to do the rest of my healing she literally did not show up for three days."

"No way that's awful. What happened? Did they send you back up without her being here or did they keep you down there?"

"Luckily I had a really nice nurse and the hospital ended up allowing me to stay with the other nurse longer until Crystal decided to return."

"Well, that's a relief. At least they didn't make you go back without your nurse available."

"Yeah. They even took some money off of the hospital bills that my family will have to pay back when I get out of this place."

We ended up talking about little things for the rest of the time we were at dinner. We talked about our hometowns, our high schools, and our hobbies. I found out he's from Durlandville, New York and he really likes to go fishing. Once dinner was finished, we cleaned up our plates and I helped him get back to his room. His room is only about eight rooms down from mine, so after helping him back to his, I went back to mine. I made a mental note to be sure that I got my phone the next time I saw Crystal so I could keep in touch with Zac and help him when he needed it.

It was quite difficult for me to even attempt to lie down and fall asleep, so I ended up watching TV for a few hours. I turned on the news and watched for about half an hour. A story covering a shooting at the Coney Island boardwalk was running when I turned on the TV. The details were gruesome but it eventually switched to a story discussing whether or not art has an "afterlife," and whether or not art can be refurbished or preserved in some way. From there it took a turn for the worse, discussing two more shootings in New York that occurred in broad daylight. Sandwiched in between those two stories was a development in the one about the boy who was stabbed by a lake with a fishing hook while he was innocently out fishing. The update said that he was recovering well at the nearby hospital and was expected to be released within a month or so.

Around midnight I finally decided to shut off the TV. I took my medications and stared at the city lights outside for what felt like forever and finally dozed off around one thirty in the morning.

CHAPTER TWELVE

Secret Message

THE ROOM WAS empty. That was a surprise because he's usually there waiting for me. I looked around the room and the colors were slightly different. The blanket on my lap was a different shade of blue than I usually perceive it to be. There was a small table next to my bed and an empty vase filled about halfway with water. After I noticed the vase, he walked in.

"Ahh, so you *are* awake," he said as he walked into the room with freshly picked flowers in his hands. He placed the flowers in the vase and arranged them until they sat in the vase perfectly. It was a bouquet of pink and blue carnations with little baby's breath blossoms as accents. Carnations are my favorite. "I was waiting for you to wake up so I could give them to you, but I didn't want you to go through the trouble of finding a vase and somewhere to put everything, so I got a vase and table for you."

"Thank you. They're beautiful!"

"Of course. Are you ready to go?"

"Go where?" Why would I ask that? Just go and let him show you.

"You'll see," he said while holding out his hand.

We made our way through the hospital and to his car. He drove what felt like forever but I recognized the area. Eventually, we pulled up to Brickyard Pond and got out of the car. He opened the trunk and there was a bathing suit for him. He pulled it out and closed the trunk.

"Are you ready to swim?" he asked.

"I don't have a bathing suit."

"You can just wear my shirt." He took it off and handed it to me.

He changed into his suit in the set of bathrooms to our right. While he was there, I changed into his shirt. When he stepped out of the restroom, he grabbed my hand and we made our way down the stairs toward the pond.

He put down his jeans and t-shirt and began walking into the water. His t-shirt hugged my body and he was staring at me as I walked into the pond. The water had mini waves created by him walking into the water before me; I could feel them lapping at my ankles. The water was somewhat cold but he didn't seem to mind.

By the time we had both gotten into the water, he was holding my hips. We were in deep and I could barely stand. I'm five foot six but he's much taller, so the water level was up to his collarbone.

"The city looked beautiful with the sunset," I said.

"It really did. Sunsets are my favorite. Mhm, wait," he said as he jumped a little, "I have a question for you."

"Okay, what is it?"

"If you could create your perfect city, what would it look like?"

This was a very loaded question. It took me a second to think of a response. "Well," I said, "I would probably want a city with a similar beautiful skyline to New York City, but without the insane amount of violence. It's just really sad turning on the TV and seeing all the violence in the news."

"I agree with you. I used to watch the news religiously but I can't anymore."

"I think I would want all-glass buildings." I thought for a second and wondered how that could be accomplished. "I don't really know how exactly that would work, but I think it would be cool!"

"That's a pretty cool idea. I never thought about that. I think I would want a city with bigger buildings than New York and things more spaced out. I think that would maybe help your design too, having things more spaced out. It might help the crime rates drop."

"I didn't think about that. I guess you're right."

The night continued on and we visited lots of different conversation topics. Eventually, we landed on the best way to learn about the human race: psychology, philosophy, or biology.

"One hundred percent psychology," I said.

"And why is that?" he asked as if he disagreed.

"Well because if you want to know the human race and society, you are looking for the psychological pieces that make every human fit into society. You look for what traits are desirable, how everyone fits into society on their own, and what effects every person's mindset has on society. However, if you want to get to know humans in general, then you need to look at the biological side of it because that comes down to the physical bodies and cells. Philosophy doesn't really need to be argued for in this situation I don't think."

"I would argue philosophy," he said. "I would argue philosophy for two reasons: One, you argued that it doesn't need to be argued for so I argued for it; and two, I think about philosophy the same way you think about psychology. The way the human mind thinks is how you should connect people into society, not how the human mind works."

The night continued like this for a while with many different conversations occurring. Tonight felt shorter than most nights, but I found myself still comfortable with his presence. He was holding me above the water the entire time we swam and words could barely describe how much I enjoyed being around him. I eventually detached from him, kicking so my body was lying flat on the water's surface with my feet sticking up. I had my ears underwater, and I was enjoying the sound of silence. He put his hand on my back, supporting me as he remained upright. The moon was shining down on us. I stood up again and started playing with the water. He was looking at me and I wanted to throw him off. That was when I spun all the way around with my hand passing through the surface of the water, splashing him. He laughed and splashed me back until I ended up going under the surface and swimming for the shore of the pond. I sat down in the sand. His t-shirt was heavy now, because of the water. I pulled the shirt away from me, suction tugging on my skin. He was swimming toward me, still a little ways away. Once he got close, he sat next to me.

"That wasn't very nice, you know," he said.

"I know. What can I say? I like to joke," I said.

"You look good in my t-shirt."

"I know." I flipped my wet hair from my shoulder to my back. "Thank you," I said while giving him a soft smile.

"I think it's probably about time I get going, though I don't want to." He looked up at me and then the water. "I like this."

"Don't go then," I said.

"I have to. I will always love you tomorrow Adelynn."

CHAPTER THIRTEEN

Familiarity

I WOKE UP TO the sound of rain tapping my window. I could tell it was going to be a very long, quiet, and relaxing day from the moment I woke up. Every few minutes, lightning would strike some-where close to the hospital and light up my room. The pattering rain was very calming. I looked over to the tray table on the side of my bed. There were no flowers.

Not long after I had woken up, my mom came rushing into my hospital room with my stepdad.

"Oh, my baby!" she exclaimed as she ran over to give me a hug.

"Hi, Mom," I said as I hugged her back. "What are you guys doing here?"

"When I heard you were in the hospital I was so anxious! David and I booked plane tickets and rushed here as fast as we could." David came around to the other side of my bed and gave me a hug. "What happened to you? Are you okay? How did you get here?"

"Mom, I'm okay, don't worry. I'm doing just fine, really."

"Okay, well how did you get here, what happened to you?"

"Honestly, I really don't know. I'm still trying to figure that out."

"Well, David and I will be staying here for a while so I'll talk to William and see if he will tell me anything."

I got excited when I heard that my mom would be staying in the city for a while. Hopefully, once I'm out of the hospital, we will be able to do things around the city like we used to. I'm really glad she'll be asking my father about what happened because it's not like I've been able to see him in order to get any answers. I held back a chuckle when she called him by his first name though.

"Are you and David staying through Christmas?"

"Yes. Harper will be coming too, she should be in tomorrow."

I was kinda excited that I would be able to see Harper and my family again. "Is Victoria coming too?"

"Yes, she is. We will all be here to spend time with you for the rest of your recovery, especially on Christmas."

From there, my mom and I spent the majority of the day catching up with each other while David watched TV. She filled me in on what's been going on in Michigan and told me about the awful snowstorm they had last week. She also gave me updates about Central Michigan University.

"Have you thought about where you would like to go?" she asked.

"I'm very torn. I know for sure that I want to be closer to you, and I like Central Michigan University, but I have also really fallen in love with the School of the Art Institute of Chicago."

"Well, Chicago is much closer than New York, so I say if you really want to go there then do it! Has William had anything to say about you going to Chicago?"

"No. I don't really talk to him. He hasn't talked to me much about college at all, or about anything in general."

"When was the last time you saw him?"

"The day I woke up."

"Adelynn, I'm sorry. That's awful; he should have been here supporting you."

Talking with my mom about my dad made me a little uncomfortable. It didn't hurt me at all—it was just awkward—so I switched topics.

"How has Westin been doing? I'm sure he's gotten big by now."

"Yes, he's gotten so big. Your sister said she has been sending you pictures of him."

"I don't have my phone so I haven't been able to see, but I'm sure he's gotten very big. How old is he now?"

"He's turning five this upcoming year."

I couldn't believe that Harper has been a mom for five whole years. Sometimes it's just weird to think how far apart she and I are in stages of life. I'm going to college and she has a whole school-aged kid. "So that means he'll be going into kindergarten soon?"

"Yes."

"Wow." I can't believe how fast time has flown by. If I remember correctly, the last time I saw him was Christmas last year. Elizabeth had gotten mad because he had his toy trucks on the designer living room couch that she picked out. Harper has kept Westin away from Elizabeth ever since.

Harper really is a great mom, and she has worked hard to make sure that she raises her son to the best of her ability. She calls the way that she parents "progressive parenting" and apparently that's been a huge trend for parents in the last few years. The way Harper explained it to me was that she wanted Westin to not have to rely on her. She wants him to know that she loves and supports him but she also wants him to make mistakes and learn how life works on his own without her telling him how to do every little thing. She teaches him about consent and bodily autonomy. When he makes a mistake, instead of her getting upset or mad she has a conversation with him about why what he did was not okay and talks to him about how he can change his actions in the future. She doesn't hit him and tries not to scream at him because she wants to show him that big feelings are okay and can be frustrating to have, but she also wants to show him that there are controlled, more positive ways to let out your big emotions. She doesn't yell at him and instead treats him like a human that has feelings and deserves respect. I think that's why she doesn't want him around Elizabeth—our stepmom stands for and essentially is everything that Harper doesn't want to teach Westin.

My thoughts were interrupted when Joyce walked into the room. Both my mom and David turned their heads toward the door at the same time Joyce noticed I had company.

"Oh my, I'm sorry! I didn't know you had guests," Joyce said.

"Oh, no worries! It's just my mom and my stepdad! Mom and David," I said as I gestured to Joyce, "this is Joyce! She is my therapist! Joyce," I said as I gestured to my parents, "this is my mom, Claire, and my stepdad, David!"

"Nice to meet you, Joyce," my mom said as my stepdad smiled.

"Nice to meet you as well! Would you guys like me to come back later?" she asked.

"No, don't worry," my mom said. "David and I can come back later! We'll be staying for the next week or so, so we'll be spending plenty of time here! Let me just collect my things!"

My mom got her purse and put on her jacket, making sure she had her phone, keys, and wallet. David shut off the TV and waited for her to be ready. Shortly after they left the room, Joyce and I began our therapy session.

"Hello Adelynn," she said as she sat down.

"Hi Joyce!" I responded.

"I'm sorry! I didn't mean to interrupt your time with your parents! I didn't know they were coming!"

"I didn't either," I said while chuckling.

"Well, I'm sure it was nice to see them, no?"

"Oh, it was definitely nice to see them! I missed my mom and stepdad so much!"

"I'm really glad they are here for you! Sorry I haven't been able to come see you for a little bit! I've been waiting to hear back from

Crystal but have had a hard time getting in touch with her to see when I could visit you again. I talked to the assistant at the front desk and she told me to just come whenever I could."

"No, really, don't worry, it's okay! I'm glad we get to talk again!"

"Alright, well I guess we can just jump into it! How have you been?"

"I have been doing okay! I'm still using the walker to get around but I have been doing really well with it. I think I will be able to walk all by myself again soon!"

"That's really awesome, I'm glad to hear you are recovering well! I see here that you got a brain scan," she said looking at her clipboard. "What were the results of that?"

"I don't know; I haven't gotten the results yet."

"Oh, okay. I see. Has your father come to visit you much lately?"

"No, not at all."

"What about Elizabeth, has she not visited recently either?"

"She visited twice after you came and saw me last time, but she hasn't come since."

"Oh wow, how does that make you feel? You said you didn't really like Elizabeth, correct?"

"It's not that I don't like her, it's just that we have an awkward relationship. It didn't make me feel too bad because I expected this behavior from her. When she came to see me, she was a day late and her reasoning was that she wanted to have a pool day and get her nails done instead. The time after that she came in for a short period of time, asked me some weird questions, and then left."

"What do you mean by weird questions?"

"Well, I had a bruise on the inner part of my leg that I don't know how I got. She asked about the bruise, brought up the car accident in an odd way, and then just left."

"I'm sorry to hear that Adelynn. I have a question for you. If you weren't related to your relatives, particularly on your father's side, would you be friends with them?"

"On my father's side? Absolutely not."

"Interesting. Why do you feel that way?"

"I just don't like how he and Elizabeth do things. Elizabeth literally does nothing with her life but feels like she deserves to be treated well, and my father is so invested in work that he doesn't do anything else with his days on Earth. My grandparents are fine and I would probably be friends with them, but it's definitely clear that we are from different generations."

"Interesting. Have you been doing schoolwork since you have been here?"

"Yes. I'm almost done with my essay but I haven't seen Crystal, so I'm not sure how I'll get it back to my teacher."

"I can take it for you when I leave after our next appointment and give it to the front desk if you would like. They could probably take care of that for you."

"That would be awesome. Thank you."

"Yeah, of course! Have you been on your phone much?"

"Not at all. Again, I'm waiting for Crystal to come so I can ask her for it."

"When was the last time you saw Crystal? I saw her yesterday, but it was very, very brief. Prior to that, I barely saw her."

"I'll see what I can do when I talk to the front desk to get you your phone back."

"Thank you!"

"Alright, so have you thought about the college searching process? I know you're a senior in high school and the clock is ticking!"

"Yes! So I am considering New York University, Merrimack College, Southern New Hampshire University, Central Michigan University, and the School of the Art Institute Of Chicago."

"Wow, that's a pretty full list. How do you think you will narrow that down?"

"I have already been narrowing it down. I don't really feel confident about going to New York University, so I would say that is at the bottom of my list. I think Southern New Hampshire University is also more towards the bottom because of how far away it is. I'll probably only consider Merrimack College if I have to. Central Michigan University and the School of the Art Institute of Chicago are my two top picks."

"Have you visited either of them yet?"

"No, I plan on going soon though."

"That's awesome."

We talked a lot about college and what I was planning on majoring in. We talked more about my family, my parents' divorce, about my stepparents and grandparents, and somehow we made it to the topic of what foods I like to eat. I have found that a lot of the time in therapy if there's nothing you can really talk about then you end up talking about random things and that honestly comforts me a lot. It feels like there's no pressure and that is my favorite thing.

I handed Joyce the paperwork on her way out and she reassured me that she would talk to the woman at the front desk about getting me my phone as well. We said our goodbyes and she told me that she would come by as soon as she could, and would begin going through the front desk assistant in order to do it.

After she left, I decided to watch some TV. I turned on the news and saw another update on the story about the eighteen-year-old boy that was in that fishing accident. They finally caught the suspect; they say that he has medium-length dark hair, is about six feet tall, and has light eyes.

Next was a story about a New York City father that got attacked and robbed right in front of his five-year-old son. Every single time I turn on the news, I want to watch it less. Following that was a story about the New York crime rates, stating that five people were fatally shot in the last four hours. That was about as much TV as I could manage before I went to dinner. It's really discouraging seeing the news with all the violence in New York City; I can only handle so much of it.

It was about five thirty when I got to the cafeteria, which I will admit is a little early for me. I wanted to get dinner early because I wanted to get to sleep as soon as possible. Therapy sessions can be enjoyable, but they are tiring.

At dinner, I got mac and cheese with breadcrumbs and a side of mashed potatoes. I saw Zac walking into the cafeteria while I was leaving and I greeted him.

I took my medications before bed and unwound by watching another show for a few hours before finally deciding to shut off the light and go to sleep.

CHAPTER FOURTEEN

———

Sunset & Him

HE WAS SITTING on the chair at the end of my bed underneath the TV.

When he saw me glance at him, he stood up and did that thing that he does where he shoots me a look full of confidence. He was wearing a black t-shirt with jeans. Yet again, his gold chain was resting on top of his shirt. He stood up and walked towards my bedside, reaching out for my hand.

We did the same thing we always do: we ran through an empty hospital, ran through the empty lobby, went across the street, and got into his car. Once again I had no clue where we were going; he always manages to surprise me.

What felt like ten minutes into the ride, I had an idea that we might have been going to the lake because these streets looked familiar. This idea of mine was altered when we pulled into a long dirt driveway.

At the end of the driveway was a little shack-type house. The house was blue with a light brown deck that wrapped it and met the end of the driveway. Peeking through the trees standing next to the house was what seemed to be a lake. Once at the end of the driveway, he shut off the car and opened my door. I stepped out of the car and as I did so he grabbed my hand and led me to the house. We walked onto the porch and he opened the door for me. I stepped inside the house to find it beautiful, but empty.

The kitchen had an island next to the countertop which had a beautiful bouquet of fresh flowers on it and a bowl of fruit. Next to the kitchen island was another island-type counter that had columns touching the ceiling on either side. About a few feet from the opposite side of the island with a column was a couch facing a TV and a fireplace. Next to the couch was a loveseat in front of a massive window. In front of the loveseat was a coffee table. The walls were mostly maroon with some beige, and the entire wall that held the TV and fireplace was made of stone. The windows on the far side of the room had an array of plants on the windowsill and even some hanging from the ceiling.

He followed me inside this beautiful house and sat down at the island closest to the kitchen counter. I followed him, sitting at the counter on his right side.

"Would you like a glass of water?" he asked.

"That would be incredible," I answered. He got a glass from the cupboard above the kitchen counter and utilized the sink that was built into the island. He poured me a glass of water and came to sit next to me again.

"This is such a beautiful house," I said.

"It really is," he said. "This is my childhood home."

"Really? It must have been so nice growing up on a lake!"

"It was. I am very fortunate. Speaking of the lake, would you like to go sit by it?"

"Yes! I'd love to!"

I picked up my glass of water and he led me down a flight of stairs next to the couch in the living room. At the bottom of the stairs was a beautiful basement area that had a couch and yet another TV. He then led me out the basement doors, which in turn led to an outdoor patio, a screenhouse, a hot tub, and a staircase down to the lake. He signaled for me to sit down at the outdoor patio, so I took a seat and he sat beside me. The sun was setting off in the distance, creating a picturesque reflection on the water.

"It's beautiful out here tonight," he said. I shook my head in agreement.

"So you said you have lived here your whole life, right?"

"Yes. My parents moved here just before I was born and haven't wanted to leave since."

"That's honestly awesome. How did your parents meet?"

"They met in college about twenty-five years ago. Both of my parents were living on campus at Rodman University in Massachusetts. My mom was living in the dorm building next to my dad's during their freshman year. My dad happened to see my mom with her friends in the dining hall and then he began seeing her everywhere on campus. He saw her at the gym, walking to classes, at parties on Friday nights, and he eventually had a class with her. When picking partners for a project in that class, he asked her to be his partner and the rest was history. They got engaged their senior year of college and had me two years later."

"That's such an awesome story."

"It is. Although I'd be lying if I said it didn't make me a hopeless romantic. What about your parents? How did they meet?

"Well..." I tried thinking back to when I was told how my parents met, but it wasn't as romantic as his story. Neither was their whole relationship, plus their divorce. "My parents met after college," I continued. "My mom was a bartender at the local bar in a small town in Pennsylvania. My father was coming from a job interview and got a drink or two. He hit on my mom and they went out on a date and got married two weeks later. They had me and my two sisters, but then the marriage disintegrated."

"Well, I'm sorry to hear that Adelynn."

"That's okay. It is what it is. I just know that if I ever decide in the future that I want kids, I want to make sure I can give them a two-parent household or I won't even attempt to have kids. It wasn't really traumatic, watching the divorce happen. It was just uncomfortable."

"I can only imagine how it would feel. I'm really sorry."

"Don't be sorry, it's not your fault." The conversation fizzled out there. Luckily he didn't allow it to get awkward.

"Would you like to go swimming?"

"I would love to," I said, grinning, "but I don't have a bathing suit." Now wasn't *this* a familiar conversation!

"That's okay. You can wear one of my t-shirts again." Without hesitation, he stood up and walked inside. Not even two minutes later, he returned with a navy blue t-shirt, similar to the one he had worn at the beach. He handed me the t-shirt and signaled for me to use the bathroom right next to the stairs in the basement. His shirt fit me like a dress. I walked back outside with my jeans and shirt in hand and noticed that he'd changed into gray swim shorts. He took my clothes when I got outside and placed them on the table in a screenhouse. I then followed him down the set of stairs that led to the lake.

The sand underneath my feet was nice and warm. I stepped into the water, placing my feet in it to see how cold it was. It was very warm, which was unexpected, but such a nice feeling. I hate being in cold water, so the warmth from the lake heightened my desire to swim with him. He was standing at the edge of the dock. I watched him. As he took off his shirt, his tattoos were slowly revealed. One was half of a bird's wing that stretched from just left of his spine and wrapped around his body to about where his arm was. He threw his shirt on the ground and turned towards me. He noticed I was staring at him, so he signaled for me to get on the dock with him. I hesitated, but a wave of curiosity came over me, and I found myself stepping up on the dock and walking towards him. I stood next to him, facing him. He faced me and began to speak.

"My t-shirt looks great on you," he said as he placed his hands on mine.

"Thank you!"

He leaned towards me. I could feel a jolt of fear run down my spine. He was making direct eye contact with me. I was lost in his green eyes. I began noticing the specks of yellow that surrounded his pupil. His pupils dilated and the yellow disappeared, revealing bands of different shades of green in his iris. He was standing so close to me that I could feel his breath hitting my face.

No, I thought. We can't kiss right now. I haven't kissed anyone since Alec and I had no desire to. I hoped he would pull away and in my head, I kept thinking *no, no, no, no.* My body was stuck and I couldn't move. My arms were frozen and so were my legs. My lips felt heavy and I knew they could not form even one word. Just when I could feel his body against mine, feel his breath on my face, had accepted that we were about to kiss and there was nothing I could do about it, I heard a splash in the water next to the dock.

He jumped.

He just created an intense and intimate moment and then simply bailed and jumped. Perhaps he could see the fear coursing through my veins, or maybe my hands were a little too shaky. Perhaps he knew what he was doing to me and intended to drive me insane.

Did I really want him to kiss me?

He surfaced, and I could feel him staring at me from the water below. I knew I had to do something. I couldn't remain there, frozen in shock, letting this situation get incredibly awkward. *No, I can't stand here any longer like this,* I thought. *If I do, he'll see the shock in my body and will think, no, he will* know *that I wanted him to kiss me.* I wanted him to kiss me. It was scary.

I need to move, I thought. *One, two, three, move!* Nothing. I *need* to move. I can't. Fine, I'll just lose my balance. I intentionally made my legs go limp, which caused me to lose my balance. I fell into the water. Luckily my feet were on the edge of the dock, far enough that they didn't hit it too much as I went splashing into the water. The water gave me back my ability to move, and I swam up to the surface.

Really Adelynn, I thought, *well wasn't that just majestic*? Next thing I knew he was back on the dock, jumping into the water. We were continuously in and out of the water for some time. We rated each other's jumps and eventually, we stopped. He grabbed two chairs that were sitting on the sand and put them right on the lakeshore. I swam up towards the shallow end and waited for him to grab the second chair. As he sat down, I could see all three of his tattoos: one on his back that wrapped around his body, one on his arm, and a small one on his chest that I hadn't noticed while we were standing close together on the dock. I sat down in my chair, and we began talking.

"The water is so warm," I said. "Is it always like this?"

"Usually, yes!"

"That's awesome."

"Yeah; sometimes it's not that refreshing on hot days, but during the night or even in late fall or early spring, it's nice. I'll bring you here during that time of year."

"That would be lovely."

We talked and talked for hours, but eventually, the warm water turned cold, so we moved to the hot tub. What could go wrong with two teenagers unsupervised in a hot tub, you may be thinking. But it didn't go like you would have expected. He got me a soda and held my hand as I made my way into the tub. We looked at the stars and delved into more astrology talk. He had his arm around me, but that's as far as physical touch went. Still no kiss.

I didn't know if I wanted to kiss him; in fact, I didn't even know if this was real. These short periods of time I spend with him only occur after I have fallen asleep, so perhaps this is a dream? It feels much too real to be a dream, however. What if I did kiss him? What would it do? If it was a dream, then theoretically it wouldn't do anything. I know myself, though; I'm too timid to make the first move.

He told me more about the history of astrology than I had ever known. He told me that the oldest horoscope we know of is from 410 B.C. He explained to me that Pisces (which runs from February 19 to about March 20) is one of the earliest zodiac signs on record, with the two fish that symbolize the sign appearing on horoscopes as far back as 2300 B.C.

We talked all night, and I knew that because we saw the sun starting to rise. Once the rays of the sun hit us, he said the same thing he always said:

"I will love you tomorrow, Adelynn."

CHAPTER FIFTEEN

Reconnecting

I WOKE UP FACING the window with the view of the city once more. The weather was beautiful, as usual. I spent most of my day watching TV, only taking a break for lunch. With Crystal not being around lately, I have noticed that there is not much for me to do in the hospital. I don't have my phone, so it's not like I can call anybody and have them come see me. I don't have my laptop, so it's not like I can get work done unless somebody brings it to me. I just saw Joyce yesterday, so I probably won't see her today, and my mom and step-dad are probably getting settled into their hotel, so I won't see them until tomorrow most likely.

The morning went by quickly as I was completely absorbed in my TV shows. The early afternoon went by in the same fashion until I noticed a lady standing in my doorway. She had light brown hair with a medium complexion and dark eyes.

"Hi Adelynn," she said. "My name is Julie and I'm working the front desk today. Joyce told us yesterday that you wanted your phone, correct?"

"Yes, please," I said.

"All right, let me go grab your phone and the paperwork."

"Okay, thank you."

I'm not a very technologically dependent person; however, I am an overthinker. My brain doesn't go far when I don't have answers and I'm confused about something. Mix that with the fact that I'm also a very relaxed person, you get quite an interesting overall personality. My mind is a racetrack, but one where the shape of the track is ever-changing.

I have a hunch that something isn't quite right. Crystal is acting weird to both Zac and me, and I need to be able to help Zac. Elizabeth came in a few times and was acting weird. When I asked for my phone originally, I never had it given to me, and Nevaeh visiting me yesterday brought up more questions than I have answers to.

By the time I filled out all the paperwork to get my phone back, it was time for me to get dinner. It was standard paperwork, such as "the hospital is not responsible for the loss or damage of the phone from this point forward," "I'm not allowed to use it to call for someone to help get me released," etc. I left my phone in one of the crevices underneath my hospital bed. I didn't want to hide it from anybody, but I didn't know if I wanted Crystal to see it if she came into my room when I was at dinner; she wasn't entirely trustworthy.

I made my way down to the cafeteria and ate dinner. I saw Zac yet again and let him know that I got my phone and I would text him once I got back to my room and turned it on.

I did all of my typical nighttime self-care stuff like taking a shower, brushing my hair, and brushing my teeth before I made it back to my room and decided to look at my phone. I knew in my mind that all the strangeness—what Elizabeth said, how Crystal has been acting, and the fact that I didn't know what was happening—could have been nothing, but I didn't trust it and was starting to want answers. I'm way too good at not trusting people, *especially* Elizabeth and Nevaeh. Elizabeth has never given me a reason to not trust her necessarily, but I feel like it's better to watch my back than allow her to ever know something I don't. Nevaeh is entirely untrustworthy and could just be pushing my buttons, but it's pretty low to threaten someone while they're in the hospital for no reason (even for her), so something must be going on.

I settled back into my room, grabbing my phone, and pulled my blankets up over me. My phone was off, so I turned it on and waited. The city lights were as bright as ever, piercing through my window. Soon, my phone lit up, shining its own glow into my face. The texts and calls from the last two weeks came pouring in. I looked out the window while my phone repeatedly buzzed.

Once the buzzing stopped, I was ready to finally see what was going on. I picked up my phone and began scrolling through the notifications. The most recent one was an email from my grandmother on my mother's side. She wanted to know if she and my grandfather should get me anything specific for Christmas or if they should just give me cash. Not the first thing I was anticipating on reading but hey, I'll take the little sense of normalcy. The second notification was from Peyton, asking me to call her as soon as I could. I figured a message from Peyton would be one of the first messages I would see. I didn't want to ignore her wishes of wanting to talk to me, but I wanted to figure out what was going on first.

The next notification was from Alec. I don't quite know how he managed to get my number, but honestly I don't even care that he has it. The fact that he has this much audacity—honestly, to find a way to reach out to me after cheating on me all because I wound up in the hospital!—tells me everything I need to know about his intentions...unless there is something that I don't know. His text read, "Hey, Addy." Terrible start. I hate being called that. "I just wanted to let you know that I did this for you. I wasn't trying to hurt you. I just want to remind you that I am someone you can trust and I always have been." Bull.

The next notification (thankfully) was from Harper. It was a photo of Westin. He had on the bright blue t-shirt I bought for him and he had the biggest grin, spreading from ear to ear. He was sitting on the carpet in her living room with his father in the background, cooking in the kitchen. With the photo were the words "Westin is patiently waiting for you to come see him again! We hope you are healing well and WE MISS YOU! Love, Westin, Andrew, and Harper." I swear, once you become a mom you text like you are writing a prehistoric letter. Even my grandmother doesn't send messages like that and that says a lot.

I kept scrolling through the notifications. One from last Monday, sent from Elizabeth asking where I was. My curiosity is growing, because I was in a coma on Monday, in the hospital. Presumably my father knew by then, and I'm sure he would have told Elizabeth.

There were multiple messages from all of my other friends, such as Amelia, Willow, and Riley. We're a group of five, but Peyton and I are for sure the closest. They were all sending messages letting me know that they are thinking about me and that they hope I have a speedy recovery. These messages make me realize that I really do love all of them and I really hope that I can see them soon.

On my social media accounts, I had so much outreach from students in my class. They were all messaging me via my socials and letting me know that they are all supporting me. I'm not really one of the popular kids at my school, but everybody knows me because of what happened with Alec. I would just say that in school I'm generally well-liked, but I'm not necessarily popular.

I opened my phone and checked for a message from Zac. He texted me yesterday and said, "Hey! This is Zac. Let me know when you get your phone!"

I replied to the text by saying "Hey Zac! I've got my phone! Let me know if you need anything!"

I decided to video call Peyton. The phone rang for about half a minute before she picked up.

"Oh my god! Adelynn! Hi, how are you?" she asked.

"I'm doing okay! How are you?"

"I'm doing okay. I miss you so much!"

"Aww that's sweet. You have to come see me soon!"

"I definitely will, I can bring the girls with me too!"

"Yes please! I really need to see all of you!"

"We will come within the next few days! We all need to catch up! Do you want us to bring any snacks with us from any local places?"

"Yes please! Could you bring the donuts from that shop that's down the street from my house?"

"Yes, we definitely can! I have to go to the store for my mom really quickly but the girls and I will come in either tomorrow or Thursday!"

"Awesome! I'll let you go! Love you!"

"Love you too!"

My friends and I saying that we love each other is something we have been doing for a few years now. One day, Willow woke up with a sharp pain in her stomach. Turned out she was bleeding internally. She was rushed to the hospital by her parents; luckily she got there just in time. The doctor told her family that if she had come in a minute later, she would have probably died. After that happened, we spent as much time as we could with her. I hated spending all that time in a hospital because of my fear of them, but I knew I had to be there for her. After she was released, we all started saying that we love each other at the end of every call or friendly gathering. We realized that any day can be the last and wanted to let each other know that we really do love and appreciate one another, and remind each other of that as often as possible.

I ignored the message from Alec and decided to put down my phone and watch some TV. About half an hour later, I got a notification from Zac letting me know that he appreciated my help and he would, in fact, let me know if he needed anything.

It was at that moment that I noticed a shadow on the other side of the window to my right. Someone was pacing back and forth. I tried to guess who it was, but I couldn't see their face, just that their hair was long and very dark. When they were turning around, I got a glimpse of their face. It was Crystal.

She was frantically striding up and down the hallway right outside my room and looked pretty anxious. What she could have been worrying about was a mystery to me, but something was definitely wrong and she was showing it.

I decided to lie down and get some sleep, so, holding my phone close, I tucked it under my pillow just in case. I took my medications and lay down, facing my view of the city. Crystal continued pacing for a few more seconds; then stopped.

CHAPTER SIXTEEN

Apple of His Eye

I'D BE SURPRISED if you didn't know how this was going to start. Here he was again in my hospital room. We left the same way we always do: He takes my hand and we leave the empty hospital. We get in his car and go on another adventure. This adventure was in a completely different direction than all the other ones were. We headed west, instead of east.

The leaves were colored in shades of yellow, red, and orange, creating a beautiful fall landscape. We drove on the highway for what felt like half an hour, going over bridges and through some tolls; then we got off on one of the exits and soon after drove down a dirt road. At the end of the road was a sign that said "Dewey Farm."

He parked the car and we got out. A lot of leaves were falling off the trees. We walked towards the farmhouse while the leaves crunched loudly underneath our feet.

We waited in a long line and when he got to the window, he purchased a bag for us to put apples in. From there, we began walking through the long rows of apple trees.

"When was the last time you picked out your own apples?" he asked.

"I can't even remember. It's been so long. What about you?"

"Last fall, I think."

"You think?"

"Yes, it was either this past fall or the year before. I can't quite remember."

The apple trees were extremely tall and absolutely filled with apples. Each row had a different type of apple tree. We passed each row, searching for our favorites.

"Cortland, Empire, Fuji, Granny Smith," he paused, "ahh Golden Delicious, your favorite!" he said as he began walking down that aisle.

"How did you know that was my favorite?" I asked.

"You seem like a Golden Delicious girl," he said as he turned his upper body towards me and smiled.

About halfway down the aisle was a tree filled with huge Golden Delicious apples. The higher up in the tree the apples were, the bigger they were. He stopped in front of this tree, placed the bag down and looked back at me.

"I think this is the best one to pick from," he said.

"I agree. I'm really short though, there's no way I can reach those apples."

"Here, I'll lift you."

He held my waist and bent down a little bit to give himself some leverage. He lifted me pretty high off the ground and I was able to grab an apple. It was perfectly round. He carefully walked forward to help me reach another apple, so I grabbed another one that was a little taller in size but still looked delicious. He continued moving so I could grab more apples. By the time I had grabbed six he had to put me down. I placed the apples in the bag on the ground and he picked me up once more so we could continue our apple picking.

Once we had about twelve Golden Delicious apples in the bag, he put my feet back down on the ground for good.

"Okay, let's go to another row, shall we?" he asked.

"Yeah, let's do it! What is your favorite type of apple?"

"Honeycrisp."

We searched for the row of Honeycrisp apples and finally came across them. We began walking down the aisle, looking for a tree with lots of apples on it.

"You know," I said, "Honeycrisp apples are very good for making apple pies."

"Yes, that's why they are my favorite. I love apple pies."

"We should make one!"

"That was my plan," he said with a smile.

He lifted me up into another tree and we eventually picked twelve big Honeycrisp apples. Once we filled our bag, we got back into his car and headed back the way we came.

We drove for about an hour straight. Once the car stopped, we were back at his lake house. He took the apples out of his backseat and we went into his house. He placed the apples on the kitchen counter and took out all of the Honeycrisps.

"Okay, let's get started! Do you mind washing the Honeycrisp apples while I get my recipe book?"

"Not at all!"

I got to washing off the apples, making sure each one of them were squeaky clean. He returned with an old notebook that had the word "Recipes" on the front of it in cursive. He flipped to the page with the apple pie recipe and began speaking.

"Alright, so we need our apples, brown sugar, cinnamon, margarine, flour, honey, lemon, sugar, and water," he said.

"What a hefty list! Let's get to cooking!"

He began grabbing all of the ingredients out of the cabinets and asked me to grab the quarter cup of cold water. We washed our hands and set to measuring our ingredients. He measured out the flour to one and a half cups and asked me to measure out a tablespoon of sugar. Then he grabbed half a cup of the margarine and measured out two teaspoons of the cinnamon powder. I measured out two tea-spoons of honey while he measured out three tablespoons of brown sugar. He cut the lemon in half and we were then surrounded by a messy kitchen with about a million different cups, plates, bowls, and measuring cups holding all of our measured ingredients. I finished cutting off the skin of the apples; he helped me finish up the last few.

"Let's make a pie!" he said.

He pulled his food processor out of the cabinet and put in the flour, margarine, and the sugar, creating a fine powder. The powder went into a bowl, followed by the water.

"Now to the messy part," he said. "We have to knead this with our hands. Do you want to do it?"

"Sure." I washed my hands once more to make sure they were as clean as possible and began kneading the dough. He turned on the oven and set it to 350 degrees. The dough quickly turned into a pastry-like substance and it was then ready to freeze.

"So we are going to mold it into a square and wrap it in cling wrap; then freeze it for forty-five minutes. We can work on the filling in the meantime."

He placed the dough in the freezer and told me what we had to do next.

"So, next we are going to cut the apples into thin slices. We can place them in this bowl as we go along," he said as he pulled an empty bowl close to us, "and then squeeze some lemon juice over that. Then we'll place the honey, the cinnamon, and the three table-spoons of brown sugar as well as granulated sugar over the apples and refrigerate it."

"Sounds good to me!" I said.

We began cutting the apples up super small and doing as the instructions said. By the time we had finished all of that, we had about fifteen minutes left for the dough so I helped him clean all of the plates, bowls, and other things we used to make our pie. We got a pan to make the filling in and took the dough out of the fridge.

We rolled out the dough and made two circles that were bigger than the circumference of the pan. From there we placed a layer of dough at the base of the pan and carefully piled the filling on top of the base layer. We lay the other circle of dough over the top and used a fork to press the edges of the two layers together, cutting an X into the top of the pie and then placing it in the oven.

We sat at the counter as we waited for the pie to bake.

"It'll take about twenty-five minutes to be done," he said.

"Awesome! I've never made an apple pie with a recipe like this before," I said.

"What do you mean?"

"Well whenever I would make an apple pie it was always apples and a few other ingredients. I've never made the dough myself, nor have I ever used lemon and honey."

"I've only ever made it this way," he smiled, "it's my grandmother's old recipe."

"Really? Tell me about her." I smiled and placed my elbows on the counter, giving him all of my attention.

"She is an incredible woman. She lost my grandfather a few years ago unfortunately, but they met when they were really young. She has the biggest heart and she is the best cook. She's just a genuine human. I aspire every day to be as kind and loving as she is. Many guys want to act all tough and empty-hearted but I just want to be like her. It's uncommon, and many people call me soft because of it, but I just want to follow in her footsteps and learn as much as I can from her."

"Wow, I wasn't expecting that response. But that's honestly incredible. You're right, many guys just want to have this numb persona, but I see much more value in looking up to someone that you care about and having that compassion for others. It will get you far in life for sure. I admire it."

"Thank you."

We talked more about family for the remainder of the time the pie was cooking. He comes from a completely different background than I do, which was interesting to hear about. By the time the pie was done cooking, I had found myself completely absorbed in his family and his lifestyle. Alec's family was similar to mine: divorced parents and a very disconnected household. I have never seen a family so tightly knit like this boy's family. Even my friends' families aren't as closely intertwined as his seemed to be.

Once the pie had come out of the oven and cooled down, we sat down and each had a slice.

"Would you like a scoop of vanilla ice cream as well?" he asked.

"No, thank you," I responded.

"Okay."

We both sat at the table with our slices in front of us.

"Well," I said, "presentation is a nine out of ten. It looks like it's cooked perfectly but the slice you cut me got a little messed up," I giggled.

"My bad," he laughed, "I'll do better next time."

"What do you rate the presentation?"

"I'd say a ten out of ten. My piece was cut perfectly."

"Of course yours was," I giggled.

"Shall we try it?"

I shook my head.

"Okay, three, two, one, go!"

We both took a bite and I instantly fell in love. The flavor was absolutely incredible. It was probably the best apple pie I had ever had.

"What do you think?" he asked.

"The flavor is definitely a ten out of ten, it might even make up for the fact that you gave me a messy slice," I giggled.

So did he. "I agree. It's definitely amazing."

"I don't think any other apple pie could ever top this. I think this is my new recipe for life."

"We can definitely make this again in the future. The recipe is as much yours as it is mine now. I'm glad you liked it."

"Thank you," I said. I liked how he said future. I have yet to figure out whether he actually exists or not. I honestly have no clue when this time with him is. I don't know if this is a dream—everything feels as real as ever, while it was closer to winter than fall when I went to bed—but him adding that we would be able to make this recipe again, and perhaps even do more things similar to this in the future, made me very excited.

"I think you know what time it is," he said.

"Oh no," I said as I felt myself frown.

"Don't be sad, it's okay. I will love you tomorrow, Adelynn."

CHAPTER SEVENTEEN

Relaxing Relief

I WOKE UP IN my hospital bed in an empty room yet again. The weather outside was quite rainy, but not the type of rain that soaked you completely and made you miserable. It was a calm rain. The type of rain that creates that warm and welcoming smell that makes you want to walk outside and enjoy the wet landscape of the world around you. Oh how I wish I could venture outside and enjoy the smell of the rain.

I began wondering when exactly I would be able to leave this place. As I've previously said, I don't mind being here, but it's getting to the point where I want to leave these same four walls. I've been taking care of myself; bathing myself, keeping up on my hygiene, protecting my mental health, and making friends. I have shown that I am capable of leaving this place; I just wonder when I will be at liberty to do so. I miss being able to draw and read in the park and spend time with my friends.

The woman from the front desk, Julie, came and visited me. She handed me the paperwork from my brain scan and made some small talk with me. She asked me how I was feeling and how I was doing and she told me what the cafeteria would be serving for lunch today.

I wasn't very excited about receiving the results from my scan, because I knew that whether it was good or bad, it didn't really mean much to me. I am stuck with little social interaction inside these four walls and I am forced to fend for myself. I have fought my way through this process and have healed myself. I have finally gotten the ability to walk almost perfectly with my walker; I just need to work on walking without using it.

The results were tucked away in a tiny white envelope with my name written in cursive on the face. A single piece of paper held my results. The top of the paper had my name and date of birth, with Michael's name at the very top. The paper then had the clinical information which described why they were conducting the scan: to make sure no serious injuries had occurred due to the car accident. Then came the findings section. It explained that after thorough examination, they have concluded that everything looks the way it should, and I was fine.

I wondered if this meant I would be able to leave here soon.

At lunch, I made myself a plate of spaghetti and meatballs. The tables were full as usual, but I found a seat more towards the middle of the room. About five minutes after I sat down, Brady walked over to my table.

"Hey, can I sit here?" he asked.

"Yes, of course!" I said.

"How have you been?"

"I've been doing well. How about you?"

"I've been good; I got my MRI results back today. I came back fine."

"I got mine back as well. I had the same results."

"I'm glad to hear that."

"That MRI was a little scary. I've never had one before."

"I've never had one before either."

"You don't have to answer this if you don't want to, but did your nurse leave you?"

"Yeah, she did. She said she would come back and she never did but I ended up getting back to my room eventually so it was fine."

"That's what I thought. That's awful, I'm sorry."

"It's okay. She came back eventually. She isn't really the best nurse but it is what it is. How is your nurse?"

"She's okay. She is there for me whenever I need anything. Have you tried asking for a new nurse?"

"I haven't. A boy that is also under the care of my nurse asked for a new one and was told no."

"Really, that's so strange. I've been in my fair share of hospitals and usually when someone requests a new nurse they almost always get one. Maybe you should try asking? The worst they can say is no."

"That is a fair point, maybe I will consider it."

The conversation died out there, but he shortly continued it.

"Where do you go to school?" he asked.

"I go to Newcomers High School."

"Oh really, you're still in high school? I thought you were in college."

"Nope, I'm not in college yet. Where do you go to school?"

"I go to Columbia University."

"Oh nice, how do you like it there?"

"I love it!"

"That's awesome!"

We kept talking during our lunch and eventually we parted ways. I spent the rest of the day watching TV, going through various stations and watching the news as well.

The news had an update on the story of the boy that was attacked with a fishing hook and the arrest that took place shortly after that. The police told the news station that they believe the attack was related to another crime in the area that they are also investigating. Following that story was more news regarding the flow of violence that this city has seen, especially recently. A man was hit by a car and then robbed twice while lying on the ground. A Brooklyn bishop was robbed at gunpoint in the middle of a church service.

The next story was about a viral photo that has been mysteriously floating around the internet. They say the photo has no original source, which is why it is becoming viral. When the photo has been reposted, it will show up on the reposter's page, but once that photo is clicked on it shows an error message. This is happening across all major platforms: Instagram, Facebook, Twitter, and mysteriously even Snapchat.

I almost had a heart attack when the photo was shown on the screen behind the newscaster. It was the photo of the rock.

I found that my thumb was staring back at me from my TV. The thumb holding up the pink rock had black nail polish, chipped in the exact same spot that I remember. How is this possible?

The afternoon flew by and it was approaching dinnertime before I knew it. At around six thirty, my phone, which was resting on the nightstand, began going off. It was Zac, asking if I could help him get down to dinner. I got out of my bed, took my phone, and, using my walker, I headed down the hallway toward his room. I got to his door and knocked. Soon after, he opened the door with his walker in hand.

I went with him to the elevator and to the cafeteria, and then helped prepare his dinner plate. I didn't get anything for dinner, but I did sit with him until he was done so I could bring him back upstairs again. We were both struggling to walk but we made do, and I was glad I was able to support him.

Prior to bed, I had almost forgotten to take my medication. I took my walker to ask for some water when I ran into Marissa. She gave me a cup of water and I took my pill. My head hit my pillow and I could feel myself getting more and more drowsy until I fell asleep.

CHAPTER EIGHTEEN

Admit Two: Just Me and You

H E WAS HERE again, waiting to take me on our next adventure. The city lights were noticeably bright tonight, as they were completely illuminating the room. We left my room and made our way down to his car. The outdoor air felt light and fresh, and the temperature was a perfect seventy-eight degrees.

We drove and drove, leaving the city behind. According to the road signs, we had made our way into New Jersey, but my guess was we had only traveled through a corner because shortly after we were welcomed back into New York via signs on the side of the highway.

We got off the highway and drove down a quiet main street, and then pulled into the parking lot of a carnival. The sign near the parking lot proclaimed that we were at the Village of Monroe Summer Carnival at Crane Park in Monroe, New York.

I hadn't been to a carnival in years. The last time I was at a carnival was before my parents' divorce. I went with my mom and Harper and Victoria. That was the last time the four of us spent time together before the papers were filed.

"I'm sure you know I haven't been to a carnival in practically forever?" I asked him, prepared to tell him all about how the divorce comes to mind when I recall memories from my last carnival adventure.

"I figured. You don't really seem to go out and do the things you used to, so instead I bring you to everything," he said.

We were still in the car, so he got out, came around, and opened my door. I got out of the car and noticed the lights from the carnival lit up his face. He took my hand and led me towards the entrance.

We walked towards the ticket booth. The sign indicated that each ride cost five tickets. He began talking to the man running the ticket booth and I began looking around at the different rides and attractions. My thoughts were interrupted when he reclaimed my attention by handing me a set of thirty tickets. The tickets were a light pink with "Admit One" on each. He had his own set of thirty tickets, so I held mine right next to his. "It's actually admit two."

"It's just me and you," he responded.

The park was nearly empty. The sun was beginning to go down and all the families and kids had gone home, leaving just young teenagers roaming around the carnival. There seemed to be only one large friend group of about five boys, about three couples that were living the high school dream, and then there was him and me.

"Where would you like to go first?" he asked.

"Where would *you* like to go first?" I countered.

"No, no, no, I'm leaving this all up to you," he said.

I rolled my eyes and chuckled a little. "Alright then, let's go to the swings first."

"Lead the way," he said.

We walked towards a ride that looked like a humongous swing set. The sign referred to the ride as Vertigo and advertised that the ride brought you about ninety feet into the air. We took off five tickets and handed them to the ride attendant. We went over to the seats and found two that were next to each other. Another couple got on the ride and sat on the opposite side of us. I kicked off my flip flops and left them on the grass, because I knew I would lose them if I left them on. I buckled the seatbelt that hugged my waist and chained the bar that went over the front side of the seat. I placed my hands on the sides of the chair and patiently waited for the ride to start as my anticipation grew.

The attendant came around and made sure we were buckled in correctly; then the ride began. As the anticipation built, so did the excitement in my chest, ready to explode out of me. I could feel myself smile with pure joy like a child. We were spinning around, going faster and faster, and that was when he reached over and grabbed my hand. I felt like I was in a movie. Weightless. I was smiling and giggling and he was as well. We had reached the top of the ride and the entire park was quite literally below our feet.

After the ride made its way back down to the ground and I retrieved my flip flops, we went on another ride which I picked. This ride utilized G-force and spins rapidly; at this park, it was called Starship. We gave the ride attendant our tickets and entered the circular capsule of the ride. We chose two spots that were right next to each other. The ride lacked any straps or buckles; it only had tall pieces of padding on the walls. We stood, placing our bodies completely up against the wall. The ride operator checked to make sure we were in a spot, shut the door, and then started the ride. The lights shut off in the capsule we were in, leaving us in complete darkness. When the light went out, he immediately grabbed my hand, indicating that he was scared. The ride began spinning and once we got to a consistent speed, the floor fell from underneath us while we remained pushed back against the wall. I was giggling uncontrollably, but I could sense that he didn't enjoy the ride because he was completely silent.

After the floor had returned to our feet and we had gotten off, I asked him about it, not wanting to drag him on another ride he didn't like by mistake.

"Did you not enjoy that?" I asked.

"I just wasn't expecting it," he said with a chuckle.

"My bad, I probably should have asked you if you were scared of the dark or anything before I chose a ride."

"It's all good. I'm not scared of the dark; I just wasn't expecting it was all. Where to next?"

"Let's go to the Speedway!"

We headed towards the race track, once again giving the ride operator our tickets as we entered. We picked our cars, got buckled in, pulled our cars up to the starting line, and waited for the stoplight that was hanging above us. A couple seconds later, after we revved our engines a few times, the countdown began. Once the light turned green, we sped off. We made our way around the first curve of the track and he was already ahead of me, taking first place. We went around the second corner and I was able to catch up to him, but as we went upwards and circled around to go over the bridge he was able to stay in first place. We went around the track three times and the whole time we were neck and neck. I would get ahead of him by inches and he would manage to get ahead of me once more. I thought I would come in second when the three laps were done, but as we came around the last corner, my car was able to reach the finish line about a second before he was, giving me the Speedway win.

When we got out of our cars I was bursting with excitement. I won by the skin of my teeth but it was so exhilarating. After that ride, I decided we should go on the Teacups next. I thought this would be a good break from the intense rides. We got on the Teacups and spun the cup as fast as we could.

Next we got on the Fireball. I could tell this one would be intense, but I was so excited to go on it. The sign indicated that the ride was sixty feet tall and went all the way around in a 360-degree loop. We gave the operator our tickets, got into the car, pulled down the lever and waited. The ride began and did a great job of building anticipation.

We started going up the circle, then came back down backwards. Then we went back up again and then back down again. Eventually, we started going all the way around the loop. We went around about three times before the ride began slowing down and ended.

From there, I decided that we would go on the Zipper. This was always a ride that I wanted to go on but never did because the last time I went to a carnival I was way too short. We got in and the cart immediately began rocking. We sat down and the operator closed the door. The cushioned bar that was part of the door touched both our stomachs. The ride began moving and we were flung forward, looking towards the ground and swinging ever so slightly. We stopped swinging and then we began moving again. This time, we were flung onto our backs and we were now staring at the sky. The ride finally got going for real and we were getting completely thrown around by the car. One second our weight would be put on our stomachs and chests, the next our weight would be transferred to our backs, shoving us against the seat. The ride felt like it was going on forever. I had quickly determined that this ride was not my favorite; in fact it was something I would probably never go on again. I sighed with relief once we finally stepped foot on the level, stable ground.

"I think I need a break from rides after that one," I said.

"I agree. Would you like to get any snacks?" he asked.

"Yeah, that would be great."

We walked over to a little snack stand. He got a bag of peanuts, while I decided to go all out and get a doughboy (with extra powdered sugar, of course). We sat on a bench next to each other while we munched.

"How have you liked the carnival so far?" he asked.

"I absolutely love it! This has been so much fun! Thank you," I said.

"Of course, I figured you would love it. I'm glad you are having fun."

"When was the last time you went to the carnival?"

"This past spring."

"Oh cool, who did you go with?"

"My mom," he said while smiling.

"That sounds like so much fun!"

"It definitely was."

We talked about multiple things from there on out. He told me more about his family and the things they like to do together. It was a little odd hearing about his family and how tight knit they are. His family sits at the dinner table each night and talks about their days. They do things together on the weekend, like going mini golfing or bowling or going to theaters to see movies. It sounded like a breath of fresh air compared to what I'm used to at home. It made me start wondering what it must be like to be part of a different family, a normal family.

Eventually we finished our snacks and had enough tickets to go on one more ride. I led us over to the Ferris wheel. I figured that would be an incredible way to end our night.

We took our remaining tickets out of our pockets and gave them to the ride operator. We were on gondola number three. It was a light purple with a seat, a railing, and roof, but nothing else. He sat next to me. We slowly started upward, and I could feel the wind from our movement against my skin. I splayed my arms out on the gondola's railing. As we continued to get higher and higher up, I looked over to my right and saw the entire park covered in rides, popcorn stands, and everything else that makes a carnival fun. I could feel him staring and smiling at me as I watched everything going on below us. I looked back over at him and smiled.

"What?" I asked.

"What?" he asked.

"Why are you staring at me?"

"I'm just admiring how happy you are."

I could feel myself blush. We went around on the Ferris wheel about seven times, and on the third, he grabbed my hands and held them. His hands were warm, sending chills down my spine. He could feel how cold my hands were and offered me his jacket. I put it around my shoulders and instantly felt much warmer. He eventually moved closer to me, as close as he could get; his eyes on me the whole time. I locked eyes with him. That was when he began leaning in.

I was feeling extremely torn. I wanted him to kiss me. I really did. The idea of it still absolutely terrified me, however. *Why am I holding back?* I thought. *Don't. Hold. Back.*

His lips got closer and closer and closer to mine. I could feel his breathing. Soon enough, his lips touched mine and we finally kissed.

CHAPTER NINETEEN

———

Messy

I WOKE MYSELF UP by jumping out of my own skin. That was definitely a dream.

Was it *only* a dream?

I gripped the sides of the bed and threw myself out of it. I took my phone and made my way to my walker. I then went to shower because I was sweaty and shaky, almost mad at myself.

What the hell was that?

It was surely nothing.

Or was it?

I shut off my brain. I'm done thinking. I made my way to the shower room, asked a nearby nurse for clean clothes and to unlock it, took a shower, changed into clean clothes, and made my way back towards my room. As I got off the elevator and looked down the hall to where my room was, Crystal was hovering yet again. She saw me and immediately tried to play off her pacing as if she was just walking one way and realized she was going the wrong direction, so she turned around and went another way. She almost ran down the hallway that branched off from mine.

I got back into my room and it was absolutely torn apart. My blankets were on the floor, my tray table flipped on its side near my bed. My pillows were hanging off the bed. The board on the wall was completely wiped. The chair under the TV had been thrown across the room near the window, and I know the chair was thrown because the window was cracked and looked like it would shatter with just one touch.

I found myself completely and utterly unsure of what to do in this situation.

I pulled out my phone, deciding that informing Zac of the state of my room was probably the best thing to do. I turned on my phone and the screen lit up. There was already a notification from Zac that had come in about twenty minutes ago.

"Good morning sunshine!" it read. "Crystal just came into my room, it only took her like three weeks lol. I wanted to see if she came and visited you as well?"

I responded by taking a video of the entire room. Shortly after my text went through, he sent back a response.

"Wow, looks like you definitely did have a visitor haha. Come to my room real quick."

I made my way down the hallway and knocked on his door.

"Come in!" he shouted.

I opened the door and stepped inside, being sure to close it behind me. "Good morning."

"Good morning! Who the hell did you let in your room?" he asked as he chuckled.

"I didn't let anyone in my room! I don't know what happened! I left and took a shower after I woke up and came back to a destroyed room. You said Crystal came to see you?"

"Yes, she came in about twenty-five minutes ago. I fell asleep with the lights on by accident last night, but I was woken by her swinging my door open."

"Did she seem distressed?"

"A little. I don't think she knew I was in here. When she came in and saw me looking at her, the confidence she had when she swung open the door quickly disintegrated. She talked with me a little and then swiftly left the room."

"What did she talk to you about?"

"She just told me that she has been super busy with things and that's why she hasn't been around much."

"Hmm, she's said that same thing to me before."

"What are you going to do?"

"Well, I guess I'm gonna have to have somebody come in and clean my room. I don't think I'll be able to do it myself. The glass on the window is cracked so someone is going to have to fix that as well."

"Maybe go down to the front desk and let them know. I'm sure they will be able to help you."

"I will. Well, it was nice seeing you. I'm gonna go get this taken care of. Thank you."

"Yeah of course! Good luck; let me know what happens!"

I opened the door and stepped out of his room with my walker. I made sure to shut the door behind me as I went to take the elevator to the lobby. The lobby looked nothing like I thought it did. It then occurred to me that I had only seen the lobby of the hospital when I was with *him*.

This must mean that *he* must be a dream. I can't think about that now though, I must figure out a way to get my room back to its normal state first.

I walked over to the front desk. There was a man working the desk; Julie was nowhere to be found. The man had a nametag, his name was Eli.

"Hi. I need some help with my room."

"Hello! What's going on?"

"My room is currently trashed. The bed is a mess, my tray table is on the floor and it seems like the chair was thrown at the window because the glass is cracked. I don't think I'll be able to clean it up myself. I can only walk with my walker."

"Oh my. I'll send someone up to help you take care of that. Who was in your room? Did you have a guest that did this?"

"No. I woke up, showered, and came back to my nurse pacing back and forth outside of my room."

"Okay. We will check the security footage and see if we can find out what happened."

He handed me a notepad and asked me to write down details about the state of my room and how I saw my nurse pacing. He picked his walkie-talkie up off the desk and asked for Jay, a maintenance guy, to come to the front desk. Additionally, he asked for Mason, a manager, to come.

I wrote down everything I saw and by the time I was finished, Jay and Mason had arrived. They asked me to take them to my room, so I did.

Their faces both dropped when they walked in. Jay began putting everything back in its place while Mason stepped out to make a few calls on the hospital phone. I sat on my unmade bed, and shortly Mason returned, informing me that they would be moving me to a different room until they could clean up mine and figure out what happened. Mason helped me collect all of my belongings and took me to a room down the hall more towards the elevator. My new room was diagonal from Zac's.

I settled into my new room and lay down on the bed. I sent Zac a text, letting him know that I was now across the hall from him. This room had the same exact layout as my last one. The board had the same information as the one in my original room too once Mason was through writing on it, except for the room number. He wrote the date: Friday, December 23. He filled in my new room number: 822. He wrote in Crystal as my nurse and Marissa as my nurse assistant and also wrote the name of my physician.

After this entire ordeal, I was starving, so Zac and I went down to lunch. We ate, and once I brought him back to his room, I helped him to his bed. I noticed his whiteboard was missing Crystal's name.

"Did Crystal ever write her name on your board?" I asked.

"She did, but one day I woke up and it was gone."

"That's odd."

I said my farewells and made my way across the hall. I sat down on my bed and tried to relax. After about twenty minutes or so, I received a phone call from Peyton, informing me that she was leaving her house to pick up Amelia, Willow, and Riley and would be at the hospital soon.

The day continued on, and about an hour later they came into my room and all gave me a big hug. Peyton sat at the edge of my bed, Willow sat on the chair under the TV, and Amelia and Riley sat next to each other on the windowsill.

"How have you been?" Riley asked.

"I've been doing alright. I just want to get out of this place honestly," I said.

"That's understandable," Peyton said.

"Oh my god, Adelynn," Willow said, "I've been waiting to tell you this for so long! I have a boyfriend now!"

"No way, who is it?"

"Do you remember Landon?" she asked.

"No?"

Amelia jumped in. "Yes you do Adelynn, remember he was on the baseball team freshman year. The one that the coach had to buy Cheetos for because that was the only thing he would eat on the field!"

I looked at Willow. "Willow. Come on. Please tell me you aren't dating Cheeto Landon."

"Guilty!" she said.

Peyton rolled her eyes. "I know Adelynn; I said the same thing when I found out."

"Dear Lord," I giggled.

"Hey, not nice!" Willow said.

"Listen, Willow, we support you, but there's so many more attractive boys in our grade. Like Thomas Hague or Dan Beniot," Peyton said.

We all giggled.

"What happened to you?" Amelia asked. "No one knows what's going on or how you've been or what happened to you. There's been rumors going around. You are practically the talk of the school right now."

"Well, I guess I got into a car accident and it put me into a coma. I must have hit my head or something. They gave me an MRI and my head seems fine, but now I guess I'm just waiting until I can walk on my own again. My nurse hasn't been very helpful so I don't really know when I'll be out, and as of right now that is all I know."

"Really?" Amelia asked. "Many people suspect Alec is up to it."

"Alec did actually reach out to me, but don't tell anyone I'm telling you guys this stuff."

"No way," Amelia said. All of the girls looked directly at me and their eyes widened. "What did he say?" Amelia asked.

I pulled out my phone and scrolled through my messages. I clicked on our text message chain and began reading his text out loud. "Hey, Addy. I just wanted to let you know that I did this for you. I wasn't trying to hurt you. I just want to remind you that I am someone you can trust and I always have been."

They all gasped.

"First of all," Peyton said, "he should know better than to call you Addy."

"That's what I thought," I said.

"Second of all," Riley jumped in, "he literally cheated on you. We all know he isn't trustworthy."

"Third of all," Willow added, "it's been like years since you guys have talked."

"That's what I thought. I don't know why he felt the need to reach out to me."

"Well," Amelia said, "word on the street is that he and Nevaeh aren't doing well."

"I assumed. I think we all knew their so-called love had an expiration date," I said. We all giggled.

They updated me all on little things that were happening at school. We talked about teachers and exams and all the things that typical high schoolers gossip about. We talked all the way up until five thirty.

"Do you guys want to get pizza for dinner?" Amelia asked.

"I'm down," I said.

"That's cool with me," Peyton said.

"Can we have pizza delivered to the hospital?" Riley asked.

"Yes, we can," Willow giggled.

"Alright, what does everybody want?" Peyton asked. "I'll order it!"

Peyton ordered our dinner and it arrived about half an hour later. Peyton helped me get into a wheelchair that she requested from one of the nurses in the hall. We left our other friends in my room while she wheeled me down to get dinner with her. In the elevator, she started a conversation.

"Listen Adelynn, I have to tell you something."

"Okay, what's up?"

"I know you don't believe in this stuff but I have to tell you this." What could she have to tell me? For context, Peyton has believed that she is a medium, or, as she puts it, an intuitive psychic, for years. I don't really know if there's a difference between the terms, or how I feel about it, to be honest. There are a few things that she has said before an event that actually did happen, but she wasn't able to predict Willow's stomach problems, which makes me sort of skeptical. Either way, I always hear her out. "I know you've been having a lot of confusion regarding sleep. They are dreams, Adelynn. I know they don't make sense but you have to trust him. Listen to what he says; he's trying to help you. I'm getting the sense there's something important that you don't know that he is trying to guide you towards. Enjoy the dreams and listen to him." She looked serious. I never told her about the dreams. About him.

"Okay," I said. "Who is he?"

"I can't answer that, he doesn't want you to know. Just do me a favor and listen to him. Please."

"Okay." My stomach churned. I tried wrapping my mind around how she even knew about him. Soon my thoughts were interrupted and the sinking feeling in my stomach was masked by hunger. We got down to the lobby and the delivery driver was standing in the nearly empty room. Peyton signed for the food and handed me the box. She wheeled me back towards the elevator and when we got inside she started in on it again.

"Again Adelynn, I don't wanna freak you out but you have to listen to what he tells you. You will quickly lose track of your life if you don't. You won't ever find out the truth and they'll walk free."

"Peyton, what are you talking about?"

"I can't explain it much further than that. You just have to trust me on this one."

My friends stayed for a few more hours and left around eleven. Shortly after they left, Marissa walked in.

"Hi, Adelynn! It's been so long since I've seen you! Most times I come in here you are passed out cold!" she said.

"Hi, Marissa! It's so nice to see you!"

"What happened to your room? I didn't know you were planning on getting a room switch."

"I didn't either. It just kinda happened."

"What do you mean?"

"Well, I took a shower this morning and when I came back everything was trashed. The window was shattered so I guess they moved me here so they could fix it."

"Oh my, who would do such a thing?"

"Well, I saw Crystal outside my room when I got back from my shower. I think maybe it was her."

"Huh, how weird."

From there, Marissa and I caught up and talked about my MRI results and how I will hopefully be out of here soon. It was then that I realized I hadn't taken my medications yet. I reached over for the bottle and Marissa went to grab me a glass of water. I drank the water and continued on with my conversation with Marissa until I got too sleepy.

I can't quite wrap my head around why Petyon said what she said. I feel like I have to blindly trust her because I don't have any choice. Whatever is going on seems scary. This feels like an intense and high-risk situation. Clearly, there's something going on that I don't know about but I don't know what it could be. I don't think Peyton would lie to me, and I just have to trust that she isn't. This is stressing me out way more than anything Peyton has ever predicted before.

I lay down and I could feel myself dozing off.

CHAPTER TWENTY

Love and Leisure

WE WERE HERE again by the lake. Typical things had already occurred. He was in my room, we left, we drove until we reached our destination, and now here we were, at his house by the lake once more.

He asked me if I would like to go swimming after we arrived. We placed our clothes and towels behind his house. He wore a bathing suit while I once again wore his shirt.

The outdoor air was a beautiful temperature with the most beautiful blue sky I have ever seen. I was so excited to be out here. After we had gotten ready to swim, I ran down the dock and didn't hesitate to jump into the water as fast as I could, while he stood at the beginning of the dock watching me do so.

We swam and swam, swimming next to each other and talking about a series of things. We talked about experiences we had as children, both good and bad. We talked about our favorite books and the books that we would sell our souls to be able to read for the first time again. I never pictured him as much of a reader, but I most certainly was not disappointed that he enjoys reading.

The sunset that rolled around had bands of pink and purple mixed with deep blues and hints of yellows and oranges. Sunsets are one of my favorite things, but he had already seemed to pick up on that.

We swam until the stars came out and even then we enjoyed the warm lake water. We held hands and floated on our backs so we could see the stars. We left our ears under the water level so we could indulge in the silence.

Eventually, we got out of the water and sat in the outdoor patio area. I wrapped myself in a towel that was large enough to be a blanket. He lit a fire in the tiny fire pit in the middle of the couches and sat down beside me with his arm around me.

"It's so peaceful out here," I said.

"It is indeed," he responded.

A long pause occurred. I began thinking about how incredible this moment was, here with him. This night had been perfect, as had every other adventure he and I had shared together. I felt so at peace that I began wishing I could hold onto this moment forever. I looked at him. He turned his head and looked at me in return as I stared directly into his eyes. My desire for time to hold still swelled rapidly in my chest.

"Do you ever wish you could stop time?" I asked.

"Sometimes," he said.

"I wish I could stop time right now."

"I wish we could too. I would gladly spend the rest of my life in this very moment."

He held me closer. He wrapped his arms around me and hugged me as if he had never touched me before. He hugged me as if he never wanted to let me go.

I was very much at peace. I closed my eyes, taking in the feelings of the moment, when I felt water droplets land on my skin. For the first time, he and I would experience rain together.

The fire put itself out due to the rain. Once the rain had picked up enough, he stood up and reached for my hand. The raindrops were heavy, yet he and I were already soaked from the lake. I took his hand, figuring we would go inside and watch the rainfall, yet he had a different idea. He took the towel off my shoulders and brought me to the grassy area of his backyard. He began twirling me around and dancing with me. My bare feet were squelching in the mud that the rain and our movements were creating. He had the biggest smile on his face. Mud flew from the ground underneath us as he twirled me around. I had never experienced such a wholesome moment as this one. I thought for sure he would take me inside, yet here we were dancing in the rain.

It was pouring. The rain was bouncing off the ground as it hit, it was coming down so heavily. It was a warm rain. A type of rain that could be easily enjoyed. The wind blew it sideways. It hurt a little when it hit bare skin, but that didn't faze me because he was with me. I have wanted an intimate and wholesome moment with someone like this for my whole life. I felt like I was in a movie.

He stopped our dancing and took me to the lake so we could get the mud off. I stood knee-deep in the water with him next to me and took in the beautiful sights around me. He reached down to splash me and laughed. He was prompting me to follow him, but I began chasing him for splashing me. My laughter was a hard and heavy, genuine laugh. We went inside his house. The layout of the house was slightly different this time. The kitchen was the same, but the couch was closer to the window. He handed me a clean towel and gave me a t-shirt and a pair of sweatpants to change into before he led me to the bathroom. He changed elsewhere in the house.

I came out of the bathroom holding his wet t-shirt. He told me I could hang it in the shower, so I hung it next to a blue loofa. I went over and sat on the couch, looking out the window at the rain hitting the lake. He walked over holding a mug in each hand. He handed me a mug and sat next to me, facing me. Tea. I could smell the herbal aroma with a hint of sweetness. Honey. My hair was still sopping wet and it was slowly dripping onto the gray t-shirt of his that I was wearing. I could feel the warmth of the tea as I held the mug in both hands. I looked out the window and stared off at the lake. The trees were surrounding it, creating a beautiful reflection in the water. The lake was nearly still; however, it was still sprinkling outside, so the surface was being dusted with small raindrops.

"You remind me of a sunflower," he said.

I blushed as I looked back at him. "Why's that?"

"Because you are so optimistic and you have a light that you carry with you. You are always so positive and you can embrace anything. You amaze me."

I smiled, unsure of what to say. I have never had a favorite flower, but I think sunflowers may be my new favorite. I can appreciate his words of kindness. I have never been described in such a beautiful way before. I looked down at my mug, taking a sip of the tea, deciding I should change the subject.

"The tea is very good. Thank you again for making me some."

"Of course," he said. "How are you doing, with healing and all of that? I guess I've never really asked you."

"I'm doing better, but I'm still trying to make sense of everything. I still don't know what is going on."

"I know you don't. I'm sorry that this is the way it is for you. That's why I'm here."

"What do you mean?"

"You'll find out."

"That reminds me, I never caught your name. What is your name?"

He smiled. "I wish I could tell you but I cannot. You and I will meet one day, and I can formally introduce myself then. I promise."

I looked back over towards the lake. I took another sip of tea and he placed his hand on my knee. I looked up at him.

"I will love you tomorrow, Adelynn."

CHAPTER TWENTY-ONE

—

Progress

WOKE UP TO the sound of the city. My window was open when I
woke up, which was odd because I didn't even know it could open.
A cool breeze came from the outside world, and it seemed to have
just freshly rained. My windowsill was not wet, however, so somebody must have just opened the window. Shortly after I had awoken,
Peyton walked in.

"Ahh, you're awake," she said. "I texted a few hours ago, at like
eight this morning. I asked the lady at the front desk if she knew if
you were awake when I signed in, but she said she didn't know so I
figured I would make you some tea if you weren't awake yet." She
gestured to a cup of tea that she was holding, and walked over to
place it on the tray table next to my bed.

"Wait, sign in?"

"Yeah."

"You have to sign in to be able to come see me?"

"Yeah, I guess I was supposed to sign in with your nurse but the
lady at the front desk said she wasn't around, so they just had me do
it there."

I began thinking about Nevaeh's surprise visit. "What information did you have to put when you signed in?"

She sat down in the chair below the TV. "Well, my name, my address, my email and phone number, and who I was coming to visit today, and a brief description as to why."

Interesting. I picked up the tea she had made me and took a sip. It was exactly how I like it, two sugars and a splash of milk. I hadn't had tea in a while, so it was nice being able to have some.

"How has your recovery been in the last few days? Any better?"

I placed the tea back on the table. "I'm slowly getting better."

"Have you tried walking without your walker?"

"I did when I first got here, but I fell down, so I haven't even attempted it since."

"Would you want to try it today?"

"Maybe."

"Alright, well, let me know when you are hungry, and I'll help you walk to the cafeteria."

"Okay. How are Willow and Landon doing?"

"They're doing fine. Landon doesn't seem to be too interested in her if I am being completely honest. I know she is excited, but I don't think that they will make it very long. I don't want to count on her downfall of course, but I just don't see it working much longer than it already has."

I picked up my cup again. "I agree. I don't think this is her happy ending. I can't believe she's dating him."

"As I said, hopefully not for much longer."

Willow really is a beautiful girl. She also has a very good heart and a good drive. She could get probably any guy she wants within a thirty-mile radius, so why she chose Landon specifically confuses me.

"Did you open the window?" I asked.

"Yes, I'm sorry it was way too hot in here. I can close it if you'd like."

"No, don't worry you don't have to."

"Okay. The city looks beautiful from here."

"It does. I'm lucky to have this view."

"I wonder what people on the other side of the hall have."

"I know one of the boys across the way, later we can look if you would like."

"That'd be cool! Hospital tour!" she giggled.

"Are you hungry?" I asked.

"Not starving, but I could definitely eat."

"Maybe we should make our way down to the cafeteria then."

"Let's do it. Do you want to try to walk without the walker?"

I hesitated. I was scared. My recovery has been something I've had full control over lately, especially with Crystal not being around. I don't want to do it wrong. I don't know how to heal my body the right way or how to get myself back to my usual state. I trust Peyton however, and I doubt that she would let me down. After a moment of thinking, I decided I'd try it. "Why not?"

I put my tea down and she stood up. She moved towards the edge of my bed, and she took my hands to help me get up. I swung my legs so they were dangling off the bed and I placed my feet on the floor. I put my weight on my feet, tugged on her hands, and straightened from my waist to stand.

I knew I could stand. That wasn't much of a secret; after all, I needed to be able to at least stand by myself when I was in the shower. Because I could stand, I didn't need to rely on the walls or the shower's handrails the whole time. It was the act of moving that terrified me.

"Alright, let's get you walking!" she said.

She was still holding my hand, which was good because I knew I needed it. She began walking backward, moving away from me. I felt like a baby trying to walk to my parents for the first time. I lifted my right foot and took a short step forward, shifting my body a little and putting the weight on my foot. I looked up at Peyton. I don't think I have ever seen her this happy in my life.

Then I picked up my left foot and moved it forwards, putting my weight on that foot. Then the right once again, and then the left. Eventually, I was walking. I still needed her hands to guide me, though.

I got about ten steps into the hallway when I heard one of the doors on my left open. We both turned our heads to the freshly opened door, and it was Zac. He had his walker in his hands, and he was slowly making his way over to greet us.

"Hey guys!" he said.

"Hey!" I responded.

"What are you guys up to?"

"We are on our way down to lunch! What about you?"

"I'm doing the same. I was going to text you to see if you wanted to come with me but then I heard your door open and figured it was you. Congratulations by the way, I'm impressed!"

"Well thanks, but I've only made it a few steps out. I owe it all to this girl for helping me." I turned my head to indicate Peyton.

"Ahh, yes, Adelynn," he said as I turned back towards him, "you have yet to introduce me."

"Oh, right! Peyton, this is Zac, and Zac, this is Peyton."

"Hi, Zac," Peyton said.

"Hello, Peyton."

"Would you like to go down to lunch with us, Zac?" I asked.

"As long as Peyton is alright with it."

"The more the merrier!" Peyton said.

Zac made his way down the hallway with us as Peyton continued to help me walk. I had successfully walked with Peyton all the way down the hallway to the elevator, and they both lightly cheered when I got into the elevator and placed my hands on the handrails.

The elevator began moving and it felt incredible. I was moving without a walker and without having to put my body through anything—what a relief! Sure enough though, within a few seconds the elevator stopped and it was time for me to walk again. Peyton took my hands and we took it slow, while Zac stood with his walker between the elevator doors so they wouldn't close on us.

We got off the elevator and walked to the cafeteria, sitting down near the cafeteria doors. Peyton had to get my food because we didn't have my walker and I simply didn't think I had the strength to keep walking on my own. She picked a meal that she knew I liked because I had eaten it many times before: a peanut butter and jelly sandwich. Peyton sat next to me and Zac sat across from us. Lunch went by quickly, but I found it interesting that Peyton was continuously keeping the conversation alive. Peyton and I know everything about each other, so it's common for our casual conversations to die out quickly, but this time she was much more chatty than usual. It could have been because Zac was there. Nonetheless, it was great talking with her throughout the whole time we were at lunch.

After lunch, we went back upstairs and I successfully made it back to my hallway without the walker, with a little help from Peyton and Zac.

"Well, thanks for lunch guys," Zac said.

"Of course, you're welcome with us anytime," Peyton responded.

Zac turned towards his room when I stopped him. "Wait, Peyton said she wanted to see the view from your side of the hall. Do you want to show her?"

"Oh, yeah of course. You guys can come with me then."

Peyton took my hands and we followed Zac to his room. We stepped in and I took a seat in the chair under the TV. Peyton took a look out the window and saw Zac's distant view of the water.

She sat on the windowsill and began talking to Zac about what high school he goes to and what he wanted to do for a living in the future. The conversation switched eventually and somehow we all ended up talking about our favorite foods. We kept going until Peyton saw the time and realized she had to leave. She said her goodbyes to Zac and helped me back to my room.

She packed up her stuff and hugged me. "I'll be back soon!" she said.

"I'll be here!" I answered.

It was already four thirty. The day felt like it went by so quickly. I couldn't believe I just walked. This is just one of the many reasons why I love Peyton.

It wasn't long until my mom and David came. They brought some Chinese food, and we all sat with the lights dimmed low watching Mom's favorite show, *The Bachelor*. I find it to be exhausting...the things people do for love. Or what they *think* is love I should say. Throughout my years I have learned that love is a luxury, not a privilege or a right.

When Alec and I were still together, I thought I loved him. I thought he was my soul mate. But I was naive. I used to be a different person. I used to have much more light and curiosity. I used to believe that people were good and you could trust everyone you meet. I turned cold after things ended with him and me. For a brief period, I locked myself in my room. I stopped meeting my needs. That was the only period in my life where I locked my bookshelf and refused to pick up a paintbrush. It felt like a piece of the girl that I once was died. I don't know how I pulled myself out of it and if history repeated...I don't know if I could do it again. When he and I were dating, I thought we would get married one day. I thought I would carry his kids. I didn't know there was a way out. I didn't understand that at any point I could have just simply ended the relationship.

I looked over at my mom. I'm thankful there was a period in time when my perception of the world was good. I wonder how she still believes in love. She fell out of love with my father and probably watched me fall out of love with the world around me, yet she still sits here and watches shows like *The Bachelor*.

Once the sun had gone down, I ate dinner with my mom and David and got ready for bed with their help. I continued using the walker and my mom sat with me while I brushed my teeth. It was at that point I realized I had forgotten to take my medication, so my mom helped me back to the room and I clicked the call button so I could have a nurse get me some water. Marissa came in and clicked the button on her belt to stop the beeping.

"Hi, Marissa! You are here early!" I said.

"Yes, I need to talk to you quickly, Adelynn. Mom and stepdad, would you mind stepping out of the room?" she asked.

"Of course, we'll go get you that water Adelynn," my mom said.

"Thanks, Mom." They left the room and Marissa sat down at the end of the bed. It was at this moment I realized she looked a little unkempt. An indescribable fear sank into my stomach and I began feeling slightly queasy at Marissa's demeanor.

"Marissa, are you okay?" I asked.

"Yes, I'm fine. I just need to talk to you about something."

"Okay, what's going on?"

"The reason I may look a little disheveled is because I've been here since last night. I've had meeting after meeting today and due to an emergency circumstance I will be switched to your primary nurse for the remainder of your stay here."

The sinking feeling went away and I realized I was just being dramatic. "That's great," I said, "I'll actually have a nurse!" I chuckled. She smiled with enthusiasm, but I could still see the bags under her eyes and a slight sense of weariness on her face.

"How do you feel about this, do you want to be my primary nurse?" I asked. Once she realized that I was hesitant to believe that she wanted this to be the case, her demeanor changed and she was ready to reassure me.

"Of course I do! You're one of my favorite patients! I'm really happy that I'll be able to care for you more; I've just had a super long and overwhelming day. I'll be both your day and night nurse but I won't be here all the time. Because I live so close my supervisors have decided that it's best if I just keep my buzzer on me while I'm at home until some other things get situated and I can come back and assist you if you need anything in the middle of the night." *I didn't know that hospitals could do that*, I thought to myself. "Oh and one more thing, we are going to ease you off this medication. I think that your healing would be better with a different one, but we will discuss the specifics of that tomorrow. For tonight, only take half of the typical pill you would take so we can ease your body off it. Are you okay with this?"

"Yeah, that's fine by me. Whatever you think is best!"

She stood up and went over to the board, erasing Crystal's name, her own name, and Dr. Burke's name. She placed her name where Crystal's was and I noticed my mom and David standing outside the room with the glass of water. I signaled for them to come back in. I took the water from my mom and thanked her. David and my mom sat down once more and Marissa came over and helped me cut my pill in half. I took the pill, thanked her, and she left the room.

Mom, David, and I continued watching *The Bachelor* until they got tired enough to head out for the night. They dimmed the lights on their way out, so the glow of the city shining through my window lit up half the room. I looked out the window and watched the city lights glisten. Time went by and eventually, Marissa came in once more.

"Hey Adelynn," she said.

"Hey, Marissa," I responded.

"I'm surprised to see you are still awake; except for now and last night, you are always out cold."

"I know, I guess my body doesn't need as much sleep."

Marissa scratched her arm nervously. "Well, I'm heading out in a few minutes, but I figured I would let you know that I'm taking my buzzer home with me, and if you need anything you can just click your button and I should be here about five minutes after."

"Thank you, Marissa. Have a good night."

"You too, I'll see you in the morning at the latest! Do you want me to shut off the lights?"

"That would be great, thank you."

She turned off the lights and off she went. The last time I saw the clock it read 2:05 a.m. I don't remember anything after that.

CHAPTER TWENTY-TWO

Ocean of the End

I WOKE UP IN the hospital bed once again. The view was that of the city—from my old room. I wiggled my toes as I looked down at the bottom of the bed. The dim hallway light was shining through the open door. Then, he walked in.

"Hi," he said.

"Hey! How are you?" I asked.

"I'm doing great, how are you feeling?"

"I'm doing okay."

"Shall we go?"

"Yeah."

I got out of bed and bent down to put on my shoes. I had to pull up my gray sweatpants high enough to expose my bright white socks so I could tie my black sneakers. After that, I stood up and we left, getting in his car and driving until we arrived at the beach. When we got there, he parked the car in the first space in the empty parking lot. We had been here before. We got out of the car and I stood at the bottom of the stairs that led to the sand and took off my shoes. He started walking before I did. After I got my socks off I ran up the stairs and across the sand to catch up to him. The sand was cold beneath my feet. The weather was slightly chilly and the sun was going down. I caught up to him and then ran past him, taking in the end of the day.

He stood about a foot behind me and staggered to my right so he could see the sun over my left shoulder. He sat down and I sat down with him.

"Adelynn, you have to trust those that have always been true to you."

I turned my head towards him. "Like you?"

"You can trust me but I am not who I am referring to. If you feel like your life has been flipped upside down, don't be scared. Embrace it. It's okay."

"What are you talking about?"

"You will see with time."

I turned my head back towards the sunset. The words he just said did not correlate with any of my thoughts at that moment, but I let them float around in my brain. I dug my feet into the sand; I could feel every tiny grain enclosing my feet and ankles until I wriggled deep enough to find the wet stuff underneath the surface.

He stood up and reached for my hand. He helped me up off the sand and we walked along the shoreline. The shoreline curved out towards the water a little, and we walked until we were standing at the water's edge. His face at that moment will be forever engraved in my memory. This hurts my heart.

This hurts for reasons that I feel too naive to understand and too tired to try to explain. I can't wrap my head around why such a perfect moment hurts. I wrapped my arms around myself while he stood next to me watching the water. I felt my anxiety peak and I couldn't control my shaking. I reached for my necklace and it wasn't there. I couldn't fidget with my necklace and it stressed me out more.

"Do you want one of mine?" he asked me.

"What?"

"My chains?" He reached around his neck and toyed with the clasp of one of his chains and took it off. He stepped behind me as I held up my hair and he placed his impromptu present around my neck, clipping it in the back. The chain was thick. I put my fingers on the chain and began fidgeting with it as he smiled. My heart fluttered, melting in a good way, and the hurt left. The necklace was nice. Expensive. I knew I had to keep it safe because it was his.

We ended up getting off the sand and going to a gas station eventually. By this time it was dark. I sat in the car while he went inside to grab something to drink. I could see him through the window. He was standing near the coolers, trying to pick out the perfect iced tea for me. The gas station lights shined through the window of the car, creating a dimly lit environment. I was running my fingers along his necklace, which was still sitting around my neck. I could feel the individual grooves where each piece of the chain linked with the next. I opened the sun visor above me and the little yellow light from it contrasted with the dim LED lights from the gas station. I looked at myself in the mirror. I had mascara on my eyelashes, but it was hard to tell. It had been there for a while, as my lashes were drooping. The rest of my face had no makeup and looked bare. The chain gleamed in the mirror and looked brighter with the yellow light from the sun visor shining on it. I closed the sun visor and waited for him to come back.

Eventually, he returned with the tea and we drove for a while. We got on the highway on-ramp that wrapped above the road we were just on. He accelerated steadily and turned up the music on the radio. It was a song I had never heard. The lights from the cars behind us were reflected in the rearview mirror.

He turned down the music to a reasonable level and his deep voice cut through the sound coming out of the speakers.

"There's something you don't know Adelynn."

"What's that?" My heart began racing. Is this what Peyton was

talking about? Is this about the rock photo that somehow was staring back at me on my TV? *There's clearly a lot of things I don't know*, I
thought.

"Don't let your mom talk to Marissa about it. You and your mom
have to play dumb. There's cameras outside of your room. Close the
door. When the officers come in you have to be honest with them
and you have to answer their questions. Your statement is the only
thing left they need. If you don't provide them with that your safety
is at risk. If he gets the chance to do this again, he'll succeed."

"Do what? What are you talking about?" My tone was dark and
strong. I felt my emotions close off, my heart turning cold toward
him. I looked over at him and he blankly stared at the road.

"I'll love you tomorrow Adelynn."

"No. No, you can't do this, not right now. What do you mean?
You have to tell me! You can't say that and then blankly leave it up
to me—"

———

CHAPTER TWENTY-THREE

A Clairvoyant Christmas

SAT UP VIOLENTLY, gasping for air. I reached for my neck and the chain was gone. I wanted to cry. I felt so unhinged. The lack of control over my life was enclosing me. I tried taking a second to relax and stop myself from hyperventilating and shaking the way I was. That was when I noticed the wrapped gifts sitting on the chair at the end of the bed. It was then that I realized it was Christmas. I am not overly religious and never really have been, but my family has always celebrated Christian holidays, such as Christmas. Typically, I would go visit my grandparents on Christmas, but due to my state, that is obviously not happening this year.

Mom and David walked in, Mom holding a cup of tea.

"Merry Christmas, honey," she said to me.

"Merry Christmas guys, I honestly forgot about Christmas!"

"I figured; with all the time you've spent in the hospital I'm sure your perception of time is messed up. David and I wanted to bring you some gifts to keep you entertained while you are here."

"Thanks, Mom. I really appreciate it! Are Harper and Victoria coming?"

"No, honey. I'm sorry. There's a super big snowstorm hovering over Massachusetts right now so traveling is a mess and they aren't going to be able to make it."

"Oh okay. Let's get to opening these then I guess." I'm kinda sad my sisters aren't going to be here, but I'm glad they aren't traveling. Victoria is working on an internship over the winter break so if that wasn't happening she would probably be here, but I am happy that she is doing something that will help her career.

My mom handed me the first gift. It was a medium-sized, thin, rectangle-shaped package. I cut through the dark green wrapping paper, and a canvas was revealed. David took the wrapping paper from me and stuffed it into a trash bag.

"I bought you a canvas to pass the time here. I thought maybe you could paint the skyline or something like that."

"That is such a great idea, thank you guys!" She traded me the next gift for the canvas, which was a smaller, thicker gift than the last wrapped in the same wrapping paper. It was a box of oil paints for the canvas. "This is great!"

"I know you rarely ever use oil paint in your art, so I figured you could try and improve your skills while you are here. I don't think I've ever seen you use oil paint before so this might be something nice for you to work with and learn about."

"I agree, thank you so much this is awesome!" She handed me another box. It was a medium-sized, thin gift. I opened it and it was a pack of paintbrushes.

"This is really awesome, I have a whole set of supplies now! Thank you guys so much!"

"Of course, there's one last gift for you!" She handed me another gift and I could tell through the paper that this one was a book, a hardcover to be exact. I unwrapped the book, exposing the back cover. I flipped it over. The front cover depicted a bright orange sky with some trees and water and a girl sitting in a boat.

"*Where the Crawdads Sing*," I said.

"Yes, I've heard a lot about it and I figured you would like it!" Mom said.

"Thank you so much guys!" Mom put all the gifts on the floor next to my bed and came in for a hug. I sat back with my head resting near my pillow and I looked at the book.

Sometimes, I hate getting gifts. Don't get me wrong, these gifts are super thoughtful and I am really appreciative that I will get to learn a new skill, but I hate people spending money on me and I also feel bad I didn't get them anything back. I took a sip of tea. "I feel bad I didn't get you guys something in return, I honestly completely forgot it's Christmas."

"Oh honey don't worry about it," David stepped in. "Your mother and I just wanted to get you something nice to help keep you entertained during your stay here, plus we wouldn't want you to spend any money on us."

"It's really okay sweetheart! Don't feel bad!" Mom added.

"Okay, I'll get you guys something when I get out of the hospital."

"Speaking of getting out of the hospital, when do you think that is going to happen?"

"Honestly, I don't know. I got an MRI not that long ago and the results came back as normal. Crystal isn't my main nurse anymore so my night nurse has stepped in full time. I took my first steps with Peyton without a walker the other day which was nice, but I'm still using my walker the majority of the time. I have been slowly decreasing the amount of medication I have been taking and I'll be off them soon, per the request of my new nurse. I have a weird bruise on my leg that I'm assuming is from the car accident but it hasn't really been getting any better."

"From the car accident?" Mom questioned.

"Yeah. I was told that I was in a car accident."

"Really? William wouldn't tell me anything so I asked Crystal and she told David and I that you had hit your head when falling down a set of stairs. When we were here one day she handed us

a paper with the results of your MRI and they said that your cerebellum was slightly damaged so that's why you're having difficulty
walking. They said the bruise on your leg was from you hitting the
railing on your way down the steps." Mom reached to the wall near
the door and picked up her purse. She put it on her lap and rummaged inside, handing me the MRI results she had seen. "See, this is
what I was given. Is this not right?"

"I honestly don't know; that isn't at all what I was told." I looked
down at the paper in my hands and started skimming. I saw the day
that was listed as my date of birth and looked up at the door to my
room. It was wide open. I reached for my cup of tea and took a sip.
"David, can you close the door please?" David stood up and closed
the door. I began reading more into the sheet:

Patient: Adelynn Grace Davis
DOB: March 29, 2001
Patient Age: 18
ID: 839027
Exam Date: December 17
MRI BRAIN SCAN
Indication: Evaluation
Comparison: None available.
Technique: With a 1.5T MR scanner, an MRI of the brain
was performed without intravenous contrast using multiple
sequences in multiple planes.

Findings: Part of the cerebellum is smaller in size than is typically normal for an individual of this age. The hippocampus
seems to be inflamed, while the amygdala seems to be abnormally small. The hypothalamus is inflamed, likely resulting in
excessive sleep.

The thalamus seems to be normal in size and has no
unusual pulsing or swelling in size shown when examining
multiple photos taken.

The pituitary gland and top of the brain stem look to be in normal condition.

The corpus callosum and cerebral cortex also look to be in normal condition.

Impression: Shrunken cerebellum is likely to cause difficulty with walking, balancing, coordination, and speech. The inflamed hippocampus and shrunken amygdala are likely to cause short- and long-term memory loss.

Signature: Crystal Jameson
American Board of Radiology

I looked at the paper intensely as it rested in between my hands. This must be fake. It was signed by Crystal who wasn't even at the scan itself, so I can almost guarantee she didn't examine the results. The terminology did not seem correct; often doctors use big words and I could understand all of these, so that can't be right. Finally, she got my birthday wrong by a day. The whole document felt off. The hippocampus would explain why I have been having difficulty remembering what happened before the accident and the cerebellum would also explain why I can't walk, but I don't have any signs of excessive sleep or tiredness.

"Mom, I don't think that this is right."

"What do you mean it isn't right?"

"Mom, look." I handed her the paper and she scanned it from top to bottom. "I mean I know I can't remember what happened before I woke up here but I have had a fine time remembering everything else. I don't have difficulty sleeping, and I don't sleep excessively. I guess the cerebellum part would make sense because I have difficulty walking, but that's the only thing that makes sense on this sheet." I looked up at my mom and she looked super worried. She was trying to hide it but I could tell this unsettled her probably just as much as it unsettled me. "Mom, when's my birthday?"

"March 28, 2001," she answered.

"According to that sheet my birthday is March 29, 2001."

"I'm positive your birthday is on the twenty-eighth. You were born at 6:14 a.m. I'll never forget that. I watched the sunrise with you right after you opened your eyes for the first time."

"And I'm sure that's true, Mom. This document isn't right. Something is wrong."

"I need to talk to your nurse about this. Where is Marissa?"

"I don't think that is the best idea, Mom."

"Why not?"

"Just trust me. There's more that we don't know, but we can't figure it out right now."

"Adelynn, you are scaring me."

"Mom, it's alright I promise. Why don't I start painting, I'm honestly super excited to use this oil paint. You can help me sketch the skyline."

"Okay," she said, still trying to hide her worried expression.

"Can you go get me a pencil? I'm sure someone at the front desk has one!"

"Sure honey."

Mom placed the paper back into her purse, set her purse down, and went downstairs to the front desk. David helped me prop up the canvas and set it up on some pillows in my bed so I could do my sketch without having to move much. I used the remote to adjust my bed and turned on the TV as well. For the next few hours, all three of us sat and drew the skyline while flip-flopping between watching the news and various different reality TV shows. By the time the sketch was in its final stages I was hungry, so David went to the hospital cafeteria to grab us something to eat.

Upon his return, Elizabeth and my father opened the door and stepped into my hospital room. The energy in the room shifted once they walked in. Elizabeth stood behind my father with a full face of makeup and an uninterested expression as she took out her pocket mirror and stared at it intensely.

My father was typing on his phone when he walked through the door. He was holding his phone with one hand and a small, poorly wrapped gift in the other.

"Hey, Adelynn. I brought you a gift."

"Hey, thanks so much!"

He walked over towards the end of the bed and placed it on top of my comforter. He was locked into whatever was happening on his phone. I wanted to grab his attention. The thing that came out of my mouth felt like a mistake as I was saying it, but once I got halfway through the sentence I knew I couldn't stop.

"Do you know anything about my MRI results?"

He stared and made direct eye contact with me. This is the most attention I have gotten from him in years. He looked shocked and scared.

Elizabeth also looked up once "MRI" left my mouth. She slowly backed out of the doorway, going into the hallway and closing the door behind her.

My father was still searching his mind trying to find the right words to say. "Look Adelynn, I don't know anything about the results."

"Oh, okay." I closed the conversation. He hasn't been here, so how did he even know about my MRI? Something isn't right.

"Listen I have to go." He held up his phone again, and his hand was shaking. "I just wanted to stop by and bring you something for Christmas."

"Thanks, I appreciate it. Merry Christmas."

"Merry Christmas." He walked over towards the door, leaving it open behind him. I heard him and Elizabeth walk down the hallway in absolute silence.

I continued working on my sketch with my mom and David. I was determined not to let the unknown something happening around me ruin my Christmas; that was a tomorrow problem.

I started painting in the background colors and my mom and

David eventually left. When they did I texted Zac to see what he was doing. He told me he was returning from the cafeteria soon, so I clicked the button to call Marissa so I could take a shower. She helped me move my canvas to the corner of the room where it wouldn't be touched by anyone and would have space to dry. Marissa helped me get to the shower room and handed me some clothes to wear after my shower. After she left, I looked at my necklace in the mirror. The little diamond connected to the silver chain was shining in the bathroom light. It projected a little circle of refracted light onto the wall.

The more time I have spent dreaming about this guy the more my life has been slowly flipping upside down. I don't know if he is real; according to Peyton he isn't. But that doesn't make any sense. How would the picture of the rock show up on the news? Dreams don't usually work like this, or at least I don't think they do.

I closed my eyes and took a deep breath to try and stop myself from thinking about what was going on. After my shower, I went back to my room and picked up the book Mom bought me for Christmas.

Once I had gotten about twenty pages in, I remembered the psychology essay that I still hadn't written. I limped around the room until I found the notepad under a stack of papers on the table next to my bed. I reread what I wrote:

Adelynn Grace Davis
Mrs. Collins
Psychology 312 - Psychology of Adulthood

Everybody dreams. Dreams are not a materialistic thing, yet they are a phenomenon that we all experience. Despite their commonality, psychologists have not been able to pinpoint exactly how or why we dream. With that being said, many believe that dreams are able to reveal a lot about an individual. Dreams are able to both reveal and reflect an individual's goals, aspirations, and fears.

Dreams reflect an individual's goals because many times, dreams can harvest what one wants and trick the brain into believing for a short period that it is living that reality.

I picked up the pencil from my sketching and began adding to the essay:

Dreams can most likely be a vessel for individuals to manifest what they want in their life into their reality. Dreams also can most likely be a stress release for most individuals. They can be a way for individuals to focus on something while they are recharging during their sleep, a reality different than their own. Some speculate that dreams can be a portal from one universe to another, creating connections between various universes.

Regardless of what dreams may or may not be a result of or what their significance is in the grand scheme of things, dreams are often found to reveal a person's desires and create a reality where an individual feels safe.

I didn't even know if what I was writing made sense, so I decided to put down the paper for the moment. I've never been speechless before, but I am now. I am not sure what dreams mean, obviously. If he is a dream let's say, I don't know what any of it means, so how can I write an entire paper about it?

I looked at the city lights and a nurse provided me with some water so I could take my medication. I felt incredibly drowsy and allowed myself to relax until I eventually fell asleep.

CHAPTER TWENTY-FOUR

The Unraveling

I OPENED MY EYES and saw my mom sitting in a chair beside my bed and David sitting in the chair under the TV. Marissa was standing in the corner of the room. Peyton was sitting on the windowsill, talking to my mom. My head hurt a little and my vision was fuzzy. Their conversation paused when Peyton looked over at me and realized I was waking up. Mom looked over at me.

"Good morning honey, how did you sleep?"

"Fine, I just I—" I paused halfway through. I scrubbed my eyes with my palms in an attempt to make my vision less foggy. That was when I heard a loud walkie-talkie squawk come from the hallway.

"Do you copy?" came through the walkie.

"Affirmative," the person in the hall responded.

"Are you with her now?"

That was when I heard footsteps come towards the door and a tall police officer with dark hair peeked around the corner, looking right at me. "Affirmative, she has just woken."

"Roger, make sure to ask her some questions and come back to the station after."

The officer walked in, followed by another officer. Mom stood up and the woman officer took a seat. She was holding a small yellow notepad and a pen.

She looked up at me. "Don't be alarmed," she said, "you are not in trouble. I'm Officer Solace and this is my partner, Officer Zimmerman, and we're here to ask you a few questions. This isn't typically how we do things, but since you are in the hospital and we recently found some new information, this is the way we have to do this."

"Alright," I said, slightly stunned.

"Do you know someone by the name of Alec Marley?"

"Yes."

"What is his relation to you?"

"That is my ex-boyfriend."

"Alright, I see," she said. She began writing on the notepad.

"And William Davis is your father?"

"Yes."

She wrote on the notepad some more. "Do you know a man by the name of Tom Ledger?"

"No."

She crossed out something on her notepad. "And Crystal was your nurse?"

"Yes, but Marissa is my nurse now."

"Alright, and the medications you were taking when Crystal was your primary nurse, have you taken those every night since you've been here?"

"Yes."

"Marissa said you have been taking smaller doses for the last few days, is that correct?"

"Yes."

She circled something on the notepad. "When Crystal was your nurse, did you notice anything out of the ordinary?"

"I guess."

"Like what?" She had her pen ready to write. I could tell that this was the information she really needed from me.

"Well, she hasn't really been around much. Whenever I did see her she usually acted strange."

"Can you describe this strange behavior?"

"One night before I went to sleep she was pacing just outside of the window behind you. I think she also destroyed my hospital room because I took a shower one morning and when I came back she was standing outside of the room and then she practically ran."

"Is that this room that you are in now?"

"No."

"And where was that room?"

"It was just down the hall."

"Okay." She was quickly jotting down this information on her notepad. "Who helped you get from that room to this room?"

"That would be one of the managers. Mason, I think his name was."

"Okay. Do you know someone named Zac Wayne?"

"Yes."

"What is your relation to him?"

"He's just one of my friends here at the hospital."

"Alright, and you hadn't known Zac prior to being here?"

"Nope."

"Alright." She finished writing and looked up at me. "When Alec and you were dating, were you ever harmed by him?"

My heart fell heavy. This is exactly what I had run from all this time: thinking about what he did to me. I was staring blankly at the officer and she could see the worried look on my face.

"Take your time," she coaxed.

"I-I-uh..." I paused and I could feel the rosacea kick in on my cheeks. Mom stood up, taking Peyton's hand and David's.

"We'll step out." Mom led them out of the room and shut the door behind her. Marissa stayed.

I took a deep breath and looked up at the officer. "Yes."

"Alright," she paused while looking down at her notebook. "Can you elaborate, please? Take as much time as you need."

It felt like she was ripping off a band-aid. It felt like she was pouring salt into a wound. It felt like she was tearing out pieces of my hair strand by strand. I'd never spoken about this before; I buried this for years. I was looking down at my hands, fidgeting with them. The words of my dream popped into my head. He told me I need to answer their questions because if I don't they will succeed next time...whoever *they* are. "Well," I cleared my throat, "when he and I dated he was very abusive. Both mentally and physically."

"I'm so sorry to hear that. When he was being physically abusive, did he ever create marks or bruises?"

"Yes. He, uhm, also when we broke up I was afraid for his safety. He always told me he would end it all if I left him."

"Okay, and is this why you stayed with Alec so long? You didn't think you had a choice?"

"Yes."

"And was he ever sexually abusive towards you?"

I was shaking. I felt myself releasing buried emotions and memories. It was all sitting in the bottom of my chest and when it came up it felt like I was throwing up the words. "Yes."

"How old were you when you both started dating?"

"Fourteen."

"And when you and he would fight, how would he react?"

"He wasn't afraid to throw things. He always had to have the last word, or punch."

"I'm so sorry Adelynn. Thank you so much for your time and for answering these questions."

"Of course."

She stood up and went towards the door. Marissa and the other officer followed her into the hallway. I could still hear them speaking. I took a second to catch my breath. My head was spinning. I don't ever talk about that stuff. The officer was asking Marissa if they could see my medical records and if they could speak with Zac. My hospital room was silent. Peyton, Mom, and David all walked back into the room. They exchanged awkward glances with each other, none of us willing to break the awkward silence. I was trying to regulate my breathing and stop shaking. I felt like I was reliving a nightmare. I looked over at Mom and she was staring intently at me. I took a second to breathe and let reality sink in when I decided it was time to break the silence.

"Mom, what's going on?"

CHAPTER TWENTY-FIVE

Illumination

I DROVE DOWN 27 East and took a right turn. It was a small dead-end road that had a view of the ocean. I put my car in park, took the keys out of the ignition, and stepped out. The ground below me was entirely composed of dirt. I walked closer to the shoreline and sat on a rock. I looked out at the ocean and began reflecting.

I've been through a lot since that Christmas Day at the hospital. Mom and David moved back to New York which has been a high in my life. I love having my mom around, especially as I am working to finish high school. I got accepted to all the colleges I applied to. I have a few more things to work out finance-wise, but my plan is to commit to my first choice: the School of the Art Institute of Chicago. Once I go off to college in the fall, Mom and David are planning on moving to Chicago so they can be close to me. Peyton is going to SAIC as well; she and I are going to be roommates. This college has everything I am interested in, plus my family and best friend. NYU was the first college scribbled off my list. After what happened with Lucas and their football team and my father, I just don't think that place is right for me.

My father is in jail. So is Alec. And Crystal. And probably Elizabeth soon. They're still looking into Nevaeh, investigating her possible involvement or if she knew anything. I wasn't in a car accident either. The entire time I was in the hospital, the NYPD was trying to investigate what happened to Zac. We ended up finding out that he and I were in the hospital for the same incident. Zac was the fishhook boy from the news stories.

After a trial and many discussions with NYPD officers, we learned the truth about why I was in the hospital. Alec decided that he wanted me back so badly that he tried to scheme with my father to make it happen. My father didn't have the energy to care enough (or say no, apparently) and he gave Alec the money to set up a scheme: paying someone to lure me into the woods and try to rob me. The plan was for Alec to save the "damsel in distress" which would in turn make me want Alec back, I guess? The person being paid off to play robber was named Tom Ledger. He lured me towards the woods but hadn't gotten me there completely when he decided to attack. Things took a turn for the worse when I started fighting back (for some reason Alec had it in his mind that I would just let someone mug me). I kept at it until he shoved me so hard that I fell backward, hitting the back of my head on a rock. I passed out cold; hence the coma. Besides being knocked out for a week, I was severely injured with bruises all over my body.

Alec was in the woods the whole time. He watched Tom throw me back and watched from a distance as I lost consciousness. Zac was nearby, at a lake near the woods fishing. When he heard me grunting and screaming he ran towards me, but Alec got to him first, slicing open his stomach with Zac's own fishing hook. Morbid, I know. Alec then loaded Zac and me into the back of his truck while Zac was bleeding out and losing consciousness. He dropped us off at the entrance of the hospital, then got back into his truck and made a run for it.

Police began investigating what happened with Zac first because he was somewhat conscious when they first arrived here for questioning. Although Zac and I showed up at the hospital at the same time, they didn't realize I was connected to his situation until they found Zac's blood in the bed of Alec's truck and a strand of my hair in the blood.

Once my father heard what happened from Alec, he bribed Crystal to make sure I was kept completely in the dark. The "pain" pills Crystal gave me every night with my Zoloft, the ones labeled as hydromorphone, were actually Halcion. I have come to learn that Halcion messes with your sense of judgment and coordination and is sometimes used as a treatment for insomnia. Crystal didn't want me to see Marissa, which is why she gave me these pills. She wanted me to believe I was in a car accident so she could profit off of my father. My bruises from the attack had healed somewhat quickly, so the random bruise on my leg was from Crystal trying to make me believe I was banged up in an accident. Crystal micromanaged everything. She let Nevaeh in to see me without proper documentation because she wanted Nevaeh to throw me off, but that plan wasn't as effective as they had intended it to be (I still don't quite understand what their plan was in the first place for that. All her jealous ranting did was make me suspicious!). Crystal was so worried about me having my phone that she tore my room apart looking for it. I was also supposed to see Dr. Burke, but she kept him away for some reason. She even faked the MRI results that she gave to my mom, but I think we all saw that one coming.

It was strange to me the way it all unraveled. I wouldn't have imagined in my wildest dreams that would have been what got me into that hospital. Tom received twenty years without the chance of parole for attempted voluntary manslaughter. Because of what Alec did to Zac, he was charged with attempted involuntary manslaughter plus aiding and abetting the crime (in other words, he was an accessory before the crime for his planning). He received twenty-five years without the chance of parole. My father was also charged with aiding and abetting. He has received a sentence of five years. Crystal has gotten her nursing license taken away (and she is banned from trying to regain it), and was charged with drug trafficking because of the medication swap she pulled. She was charged with plenty more, way more than I can think of off the top of my head, and she has also received twenty-five years without the chance of parole. Elizabeth is still under questioning.

Zac and I have remained friends and we check in on each other every once in a while. We went through the recovery process together without even really recognizing that we were in the same place for the same reason, yet we have split ways and are going on to live our own adventures. With that being said, Peyton and Zac have been talking a lot lately, and I think some romance might be sparking between the two of them.

My recovery went pretty quickly after I was eased off the wrong medication and given the chance to rest and heal. Mom and David spent a lot of time with me in the hospital and I did get to complete my oil painting. The bruise on my leg has gone away and I have had a great sleep schedule. I can even walk without a walker!

I am going to be graduating in about two months and am already sifting through graduation cap ideas. I want to do something that has a sunflower on it to represent optimism and strength. It's looking like I am going to graduate high school with a 3.4 GPA, which is not that bad considering all I have been through in the last four years.

As I inch closer and closer to graduation, I have decided that I do not want to bring all this baggage from being in the hospital—and more importantly the baggage of what Alec did to me in high school—with me to college. Joyce is still my therapist and I have been meeting with her weekly. I finally took full advantage of the opportunity, and found the strength to talk about what Alec did to me at such a young age.

Marissa and I still keep in touch via email and I talk with her every once in a while. I could not be more appreciative of what she did for me towards the end of my days at the hospital, as she really took care of me and she was the only reason I healed as quickly as I did.

I looked out at the shoreline where the water met the sky. I could feel the wind blowing in my hair. I stood up and got off the rock, getting back in my car and making my way onto the highway. I connected to my radio via bluetooth, put on my favorite song, and began driving.

I haven't seen him since. I convinced myself that he was a dream because of what Peyton said and because that is the only logical thing I can think of. I don't dream at all anymore actually, which is surprising.

They say that letting go is always necessary. When something is in your life that is no longer yours, you are always advised to let go of it. Find new adventures to explore. Erasing him from my mind has been the most difficult thing I have had to come to terms with. The ghost of him lingers in my life. I wish I could change it, or explain it in better terms. No matter how hard I try not to think about the mystery of him, I am always led back to the same adventures. I still don't know his name or who he is. Sometimes I drive past Brickyard Pond on my way to the market, and I can't help but think about the time we visited there. I can't go to the beach without seeing a pink and gray rock and being reminded of the photo he took. I know allowing the ghost of him to linger is dangerous, but it's a danger that I simply cannot escape.

I don't mind that I no longer see him, yet there have been many tomorrows since I last saw his face. I try not to think about it, but when I do I wonder about the significance of him and the words he said. Days pass and months go by, tomorrow comes and then subsides. Yet, every once in a while I still wonder what my perception of the world would be like if he was still here to tell me that he'll love me tomorrow.

The End

ACKNOWLEDGMENTS

———

WORKING ON THIS book has been an incredible adventure, but I could not have done it without my support system. Putting this section in this book cannot even begin to describe how thankful I am for all of these people, but they definitely deserve the recognition because this book would not have been written and published if they did not support me every step of the way.

Thank you to Shanna for constantly putting up with my ideas, going to publishing meetings with me, helping me build the plotline of the book, taking my promotional photos, and so much more. There is no doubt in my mind that I wouldn't have been able to do this without you.

Thank you to Tyler for supporting me endlessly and always picking up my calls. You never fail to remind me that I could do anything I set my mind to and without your support, I know this wouldn't have been possible.

Thank you to my family (most importantly my Mom and Dad) and my closest friends (Jami, Hannah, Sara, and Sam). Mom, you gave me your sense of creativity and Dad, you gave me your ability to be super passionate about anything and everything I do. Jami, Hannah, Sara, and Sam, you have all watched me grow up both in my professional and personal life. I have loved living life alongside you all. For years all of you have supported me endlessly in every single area of my life. You have all helped shape the woman and author I am today.

Thank you to Charlene, who showed me the importance of being an educated woman. Not many people would believe that I struggled in elementary school. You helped turn that around and you are not only the reason I am in college but also the reason I like educating myself and expanding my horizons, which is something I desperately needed to be able to do to write and publish this book.

Thank you to Dawn and Steven from Stillwater River Publications. When I first met with you in July of 2022, I had been turned down and belittled by so many other publishing companies. You were the people that believed in me and my book and you have supported me through every step of this process which has been so relieving and has fueled my passion.

Thank you to all of those who reached out to congratulate me and express your excitement for this book's release. That has meant more to me than you will ever know.

Yeah, publishing a book is pretty awesome, but having you all in my life makes my life so much more valuable. I love all of you.

ABOUT THE AUTHOR

KATELYN SIMEONE is a student attending Roger Williams University. Katelyn is studying Elementary Education and has had this as her declared major since she committed to Roger Williams University in 2021. Despite following this career path, Katelyn has always had a passion for writing and has dreamed of writing her own book.

It wasn't until the spring of 2021 that Katelyn decided that she wanted to begin writing her own book. She was about to graduate high school at this point in time and was facing many stressors due to this, as well as suffering in the midst of a breakup. With all of this combined, Katelyn reached out to her friends asking them for book plot ideas. Combining many of their ideas and her own together, *Love You Tomorrow* was born.

It took Katelyn a year and a half to finish writing this book, with many breaks taken in between this time to focus on her academics. In the summer of 2022, Katelyn decided to meet with a publisher to jumpstart the process of publishing the book despite the book still being in the writing process. This was around the time that Katelyn opened her book-themed TikTok account (@katelyn_writes) to gain a following and document her experience of writing a book.

Katelyn finished this book in the winter of 2022 and has begun writing another book.